TO our dear frien H R
I know thy works:
Behold I have set
before thee an
open door and
no man shall shut it:
For thou hast a little
strength and hast not
denied my Name.
Rev. III. 8

BY MARGUERITE DE ANGELI

A YEARLING BOOK

Published by
Bantam Doubleday Dell Books for Young Readers
a division of
Bantam Doubleday Dell Publishing Group, Inc.
1540 Broadway
New York, New York 10036

ISBN: 0-440-22740-2

Previous Yearling edition

Reprinted by arrangement with Doubleday Books for Young Readers

Printed in the United States of America

June 1997

10 9 8 7 6 5 4 3 2 1

OPM

INTRODUCTION

As always, Mama was astonished that anyone would think her work superior enough to win the Newbery Medal. To say she was thrilled would be an understatement. Typically, she gave a great deal of credit to an old friend, Harm Robinson, who was the inspiration for THE DOOR IN THE WALL, and to her editor at Doubleday, Peggy Lesser (Mrs. Norman Foster).

Her sense of wonder and modesty about her talent were things that lent her work such charm, in both the text and the illustrations, and her love of people, especially children, is evident throughout.

—Ted de Angeli
1989

ROBIN drew the coverlet close about his head and turned his face to the wall. He covered his ears and shut his eyes, for the sound of the bells was deafening. All the bells of London were ringing the hour of Nones. St. Mary le Bow was nearest, St. Swithin's was close by, and not far away stood great St. Paul's. There were half-a-dozen others within sound, each clamoring to be heard. It seemed to Robin as if they were all inside his head screaming to be let out. Tears of vexation started to his eyes, but he held them back, for he remembered that a brave and "gentil" knight does not cry.

Ever since he could remember, Robin had been told what was expected of him as son of his father. Like other sons of noble family, he would be sent away from his mother and father to live in the household of another knight, where he would learn all the ways of knighthood. He would learn how to be of service to his liege lord, how to be courteous and gentle, and, at the same time, strong of heart.

Robin thought of his father and how he had looked on that last day when he rode off to the Scottish wars at the head of the column. Now, remembering, Robin could almost feel the weight of his father's mailed glove on his shoulder as he said good-by. Then he had been straight and strong, standing there in the courtyard as the men rode forth.

"Farewell, my son," his father had said, "forget not to be brave. God knows when we shall meet again. Farewell."

He must not cry.

Robin thought of his mother and how she, too, had said farewell, the day after his tenth birthday. She had called him to her side in the solar where she sat weaving.

"Since your father left for the wars, it has been a comfort to have you near," she said, "but you are ten and no longer a child to be looked after by womenfolk. It is time now for you to leave me. John-the-Fletcher will come for you in a few days and will take you to Sir Peter de Lindsay, as we have arranged. There, too, you will be away from danger of the plague, which seems to be spreading. And now it is fitting that I obey the wish of the Queen to be her lady in waiting, for she is in need of my care. Today an escort will be sent for me and I shall go. Jon-the-Cook, Gregory, and Dame Ellen will serve you until John-the-Fletcher arrives. Farewell, my son. Be brave."

She had drawn Robin to her and had turned away so he would not see her tears.

Little did she know how much Robin would need her! For the very next day he had become ill and unable to move his legs. That had been more than a month ago.

He was cold. He wished Ellen would come to mend the fire.

The bells stopped ringing, and Robin heard the boys from the Brothers' School running and shouting along the street. He hoped that William or John, Thomas or Roger would come in to tell him the news, but when their voices grew faint, he knew they had gone on past.

How he wished he were with them. Even the tiresome lessons of singing and reading would be worth doing if only he could run down the street with the other boys.

But he could not run. He couldn't even get out of bed.

Because he was unable to see out of the wind hole (window) Robin had learned to guess at what was going on down in the street. He knew the sound of armor and knightly equipment, for the King's men passed that way going to and from the Tower or Westminster, to joust or tournament, to parade, or on business for the King. A horse was passing now, but Robin was sure it was not of that order. It was probably the shire reeve's horse, for above the slow clatter over the cobbles Robin could hear the grating of runners on a kind of sled the horse was dragging. From the odor that came through the window he could guess that Wat Hokester had been taken again for selling putrid fish in the market stall.

Robin chuckled. He knew that soon Wat would be standing in the stocks near the fish market with his evil-smelling goods hanging from his neck.

Now Robin heard the sound of Dame Ellen's feet shuffling along the passage to his wall chamber.

He turned his head to see what kind of dish she carried, but quickly looked away again when he saw that it was a bowl with steam rising from it. Was it barley soup? Was it a stew of rabbit? He didn't know and didn't care. The thought of it was all mixed with the sickening odor that came up with the raw wind from the street.

Ellen's skirt brushed the bed as she leaned toward Robin. She was near enough so he could hear the creak of her starched linen coif as she peered at him to see whether he was asleep. He shut his eyes so as not to see the great whiskered wart on her chin, and tried to close his ears to the sound of her Cockney speech. She saw by the squinching of his eyes that he was awake.

"Turn over, do, there's a good lad," she said, intending her voice to be soft, but it was not. It sounded harsh and flat, "as if her mouth had been stretched too wide," thought Robin. He shook his head and closed his mouth tight against the food.

"Wilt not have this good porridge all with honey spread?" Ellen's coaxing voice went on. Robin shuddered, and buried his face in the cushion.

If only his lady mother were here. She would have seen to it that the porridge had been smoothly cooked and salted. She would speak in her gentle way with the pleasant mixture of Norman French and good English words that were becoming the fashion. If only she were here, all would be well. The damp, sweaty feeling would leave his head, his legs would obey him and take him where he wanted to go, racing up and down alleyways or along the high street. He would be running with the boys down Pudding Lane or across London Bridge, playing tag among the shops.

But his legs would not obey him. They were like two long pieces of uncooked dough, he thought, such as Jon-the-Cook rolled out on his molding board.

Ellen tugged gently at the coverlet.

"Sweet lad," she begged, " 'twill give thee strength and mend those ailing limbs."

Robin would neither turn nor answer. Let her take the sickening stuff away. Let her throw it into the street on top of that fishmonger who had just gone past.

"Come, my pretty——" But Ellen got no further with her wheedling. Robin gathered all his strength and flung his arm toward the bowl of porridge, sending it flying out of Ellen's hands and spreading its contents all over her. He was ashamed as soon as he had done it, but Ellen did look funny with the mess hanging from her chin.

"Wicked boy!" she cried. "No more will I serve thee.

Scarce able to stand have I been this day, yet have I been faithful. But I am a free woman and can go my way. Just wait and see when more victuals are brought thee! Ungrateful wretch!" She burst into loud weeping and left the room, wiping the porridge off with her apron. Robin turned again to the wall. "She will come back," he thought, "as she has done before, and she had better bring something I like if she wants me to eat it."

But she didn't come back. An hour went by. Then another hour. It grew colder and colder.

Robin examined for the hundredth time the carvings on the hammer beams supporting the roof of the hall. Each one was an angel with feathered wings. He studied one by one the grotesque carvings of dwarfs that decorated the roof bosses, and the corbels finishing the doorway. He wearied of thinking about them and wished that Ellen would come.

Robin's bedchamber was off the main hall or living room of the house, in an embrasure of the thick wall. Like the hall, Robin's room was somewhat chapel-like, for the houses of the time of Edward the III of England were very little different from churches.

Afternoon sounds came into the room: people passing along the street to and from the shops in Cheapside or Poultry Lane; carters carrying goods to the wharves on the Thames, Belinsgate, or Queen Hythe. He heard children playing games, hoodman-blind and hide-and-seek. He wished he could have been among them, because he knew a secret nook where he always hid and where he was seldom discovered. It was down Honey Lane in the angle of a jutting wall near Black Friars entry. It was so small a space that it appeared to be no space at all. It was still his own secret.

Robin tried very hard to get out of bed so he might look

out of the window, but he only fell back again onto the pillow exhausted from the effort. Hunger bit at his empty stomach. He was hungry enough now to have eaten the porridge Ellen had brought him.

He listened, hoping to hear her footsteps in the passage, but the house was strangely silent. No sound of talk or laughter came from the hall, for most of the servants and retainers had gone either with his father, Sir John de Bureford, or with his mother, the Lady Maud. Robin called for Ellen, and when he had no answer, called for Jon-the-Cook, then for old Gregory, the gardener.

He listened again, holding his breath, but he heard no one, and saw not a soul from Nones to Vespers, when the bells began to ring again.

He was alone.

Just as the bells stopped ringing Robin heard a noise as of a door opening. Then someone mounted the stair and came along the passage. Perhaps it was one of the boys; but not likely, for whoever it was walked rather slowly instead of running, as William or Thomas or John would have done.

The footsteps turned toward the chamber. In the doorway stood a monk with a basket. He came toward the bed where Robin lay.

"Good eve, my son," he said. "I am Brother Luke, a wandering friar, newly come to St. Mark's. I have brought thee food, and, cause 'tis Friday, fish."

Fish! Robin's stomach took a sudden turn. But a good smell came from the covered basket Brother Luke carried, and he was hungry. So he smiled a welcome, and the friar explained how he had happened to know that Robin needed help.

"A poor widow, who twice a week is fed from our hospice, told me of thy need. She said that Dame Ellen, who

lately served thee, has this very day been taken of the plague. She it was who told us that all thy servants, too, are fled, because of the plague, and some are dead of it. Dame Ellen told thee not, pitying thee. Now, be a good lad and take thy supper."

He obediently ate what the friar fed him.

When he was fed, Brother Luke, who had talked quietly the while, fetched water in a basin, washed him, and in other ways made him comfortable. He took the rumpled sheets off the bed, then sat down to rub Robin's legs and back. While he rubbed, he spoke.

"It is well known that thy noble father hath of his goodness given money to St. Mark's. So to St. Mark's I'll take thee, and will care for thee in mine own quarters, because all other beds and places are already taken by those in the parish who have great need. Even the corridors are filled and the cloisters lined with pallets."

"But I cannot walk," said Robin woefully. "See you, my two legs are as useless as if they were logs of wood. How shall I go there? My father is with the King at the Scottish wars, and with him are all his men at arms. My lady mother has been commanded to attend upon Her Majesty the Queen. It is supposed by them that I am now page in the household of Sir Peter de Lindsay at his castle in the north. John-the-Fletcher was to have come for me in March, before the Feast of St. Gregory. Instead, a messenger came on that day to say that he had been set upon by thieves and lay wounded in the hospice at Reading. He came later to fetch me, but found me thus, unable to walk or ride. He brought a surgeon who said I had not the plague but some other malady. He told Ellen to feed me well and that he would return. He came not again nor did John-the-Fletcher."

"Alas," said Brother Luke sadly, "because of the plague

all the physicians are working night and day. Either he himself has been taken or he has been so busy caring for others he has not been able to return. As for John-the-Fletcher, he may have gone out the city gate and not been allowed to re-enter, for they are keeping strangers out now. Fear not for the manner of our going to St. Mark's. Tethered in the courtyard is a jennet ready saddled with blankets whereon thou'lt ride softly. Walking beside thee, I shall support thee, and so we shall go through Knightrider Street and Giltspur to Ludgate and then toward Smoothfield where stands St. Mark's. Dost remember the long wall that is about the garden of thy father's house?"

"Yes," said Robin, "of course. Why?"

"Dost remember, too, the wall about the Tower or any other wall?" Robin nodded. "Have they not all a door somewhere?"

"Yes," said Robin again.

"Always remember that," said the friar. "Thou hast only to follow the wall far enough and there will be a door in it."

"I will remember," Robin promised, but he wasn't sure that he knew what Brother Luke meant to say.

While he was speaking, the friar had been caring for Robin, easing his tired muscles, and making him clean and comfortable. He opened a large chest and found underlinen and hosen, a hood with a long peak, and a warm cloak.

"The evening damp creeps up from the Thames," said the friar, pulling the hosen over Robin's shrunken legs, "and though the days are longer now, it is still early in the season. Good English wool will keep thee warm. Now for the hood." He pulled the hood down over Robin's head and settled it around his shoulders while he held him against his coarse-woven monk's frock.

Then Brother Luke put his strong arms under Robin, hoisted him onto his back, carrying the bundle of Robin's clothes and the basket in one hand and steadying Robin with the other. Down they went through the great echoing hall, down the winding stair at the other end past the empty kitchens, and out into the courtyard. There stood the little Spanish horse, Jenny, just as Brother Luke had said, patiently waiting.

Brother Luke set Robin on the jennet, the robe and blankets around him making him comfortable. Brother Luke put a strap around Robin's waist, then ran it under the jennet's belly to keep him from falling. He tied the bundle on at the back, and they set forth.

Out through the door in the wall of the courtyard they went, into the street, Robin leaning against Brother Luke, and the jennet picking her way sedately over the cobbles.

There were not many people abroad, for it was the end of the day. Curfew was ringing as they turned up Creed Lane to Ludgate Hill, and only because the guard knew Brother Luke's habit were they allowed to pass through the city gate. By then they were more than halfway to the hospice, but it was nearly dark when they reached St. Mark's and were admitted by the porter at the postern gate.

"Will I go back home soon?" asked Robin fearfully, for the gate had clanged shut behind them as if it had been closed forever. "Will a message be sent to my father? Or to my mother?"

"Be comforted, my child," Brother Luke answered. "As soon as the plague is somewhat quieted in London, a messenger will be sent to thy father. Meanwhile, we shall care for thee." He lifted Robin and carried him to his own cell and put him on the narrow cot. "Now, rest, my son," he said.

MAY came in with a burst of bloom in hedge and field. There was hawthorn both pink and white, and primroses and buttercups carpeted the fields with yellow. In every garden wallflowers blossomed in bright color and filled the air with perfume.

For days Robin was cared for as if he were a little child. Brother Luke brought him food, kept him washed, and changed his clothes, but he was too much occupied with other things to stay with Robin for very long at a time. The bells clamored as loudly as ever, but now the sound was associated with the regular procession of the monks going to devotions. Robin grew to like it.

He began to sleep well on the hard cot and to feel at home in the little cell. He could see nothing but the sky through the small wind hole, for it was high in the stone wall and only in the early morning allowed a ray of sunshine to come in. Against another wall stood a prayer stool and desk combined, with a smaller one beside it. On the wall hung a little cupboard which held Brother Luke's few personal belongings and his breviary.

Robin couldn't see into the corridor, and at first couldn't identify all the sounds he heard. He liked the "s-s-sh-shing" sound of feet on stone, as the monks passed to and fro. Sometimes, when they passed in procession, chanting, he joined in

the singing, for most of the plain songs were known to him. Sometimes there were long silences, when he heard nothing but the mewing of the cat Millicent, or the squeaking of a mouse she had caught.

There were hundreds of people within the hospice, but they were separated by thick walls and long passages. The outer court was far away at the other side of the monastery. There, visiting pilgrims, knights at arms, merchants, and minstrels gathered, each awaiting the attention of the Prior. Because there were few inns, the monasteries were open for the entertainment of wayfarers, rich and poor alike. Besides that portion reserved for travelers there was an almonry overflowing with the poor of London, seeking food and clothing. St. Mark's was a busy place. But most of the activity was far away from Robin. He was much alone, and time seemed long.

One day Brother Luke said, "It is time now to try thee

sitting up." He was rubbing Robin's legs as he did every day, talking the while. "If thy hands are busy, time will pass more quickly. Dost like to whittle?"

"Of course," answered Robin. "Who does not? But I have nought to whittle."

"I shall find thee a piece of soft pine and will lend thee my knife. 'Tis sharp and of good steel. This bench will fit against thy back to support thee." Brother Luke set the oaken bench at Robin's back and fitted a cushion for his comfort.

"Can I make a boat?" asked Robin. "Can I make it now?"

Brother Luke nodded and left the cell. It seemed long before he returned.

Finally he brought the knife and the piece of pine he had promised. It felt smooth and clean to Robin's hands, and he liked to watch the small white shavings peel off. At first he scarcely knew where to begin to bring out the shape of a boat, but little by little it began to round out and at one end a point began to appear, as if it had been a prow.

"Perhaps I can make it into a sailing boat like the fishermen bring to Belin's gate, or a barge such as the King uses," he said. "Perhaps when it is done I will be able to walk, and can go to the Thames to sail it."

"Perhaps," agreed the friar. It was very exciting, but Robin had to stop often to rest.

Brother Luke brought soup in which dark bread was to be sopped. Robin didn't want any of it. He wanted only to go on with his whittling, and turned away from the food.

"But 'tis made of good mutton in which bay and marigold have been seethed," Brother Luke coaxed. "Brother Michael grows these fragrant herbs in the garden. Bay is tasty and gives good appetite; marigold is said to be of value against poor sight and angry words. It is said 'twill draw evil humors out of the head, and the flowers make fair garlands for maidens because of their golden color."

What cared Robin for garlands for maidens? What cared he for fragrant herbs? Soppy food he despised. Brother Luke looked patient, said nothing, but continued to hold the food ready, and Robin gave in. He drank the soup and ate the bread dry.

Because he had something interesting to do and to think about, Robin found the days passing more quickly. He began to recognize sounds as he had done before, and to associate footsteps and differing gaits with the people to whom they belonged. Now and then one of the monks would look in on Robin to give him cheer or to say an Ave, so he knew several of the monks by name, and could tell which of them was passing. Brother Andrew he knew, because he dragged one foot a little. Brother Thomas walked very swiftly: heel and toe, heel and toe, whistling tunelessly under his breath as he went. Brother Paul was a large man, and when he walked through the corridor the thudding of his feet seemed to shake the walls, heavy as they were. Besides, one of his shoes squeaked.

Robin worked steadily at his little boat. He finished the hull on the fourth day of the second week.

"I see this is to be a sailing boat after all, instead of a barge," said Brother Luke. "It is somewhat awry, with the bow aslant from the stern, but it hath an air, as if it had been battling the storm."

Brother Luke brought small slender pieces of pine and showed Robin how to smooth them into mast and bowsprit, then found scraps of linen for sails and pieces of yarn for rigging. He even begged a scrap of silk ribbon from a traveler for Robin to use as a pennant for the masthead. As if the toy boat had belonged to the King's fleet, Robin thought.

Never before had Robin done anything of the kind for himself. Always one of his father's retainers had made what toys he had. Once Rolfe had made him a hobbyhorse, and once Elfred the Dane had made him a boat, but it had not seemed so fine as this one. Now, he could hardly wait to begin something else. He would like to carve one of those dwarfs, for example, such as those in the roof bosses in his father's house. Brother Luke suggested something easier.

"Patience, my son," he said. "It takes great skill to carve figures like that. Why not make a simple cross? 'Twill be fit to hang over thy cot if 'tis well made and smoothly finished. I'll find some pieces of wood and will show thee how to begin." Always while Brother Luke talked he rubbed away at Robin's legs, then turned him and smoothed his back.

Busy as he was, Brother Luke found time to bring Robin the pieces of wood he had promised.

"These I saved from the pruning of the walnut tree that stands by the well," he said. "It is weathered, for it hath lain in sun and rain these many months."

"And how shall I fasten the pieces of the cross together?" asked Robin. "Shall I nail it then? Or how shall it be done?"

"When thou'rt ready for that, Brother Matthew will show thee," answered the friar. "Now make it smooth and fine, and have it well proportioned, for it will be a keepsake and not a toy like the little boat. That I leave to thy judgment, for 'tis part of the joy in making things."

Each day the pieces of the cross grew smoother and better shaped, for Brother Luke would examine them and show how they were too wide here or too uneven there.

Each day, too, Robin grew stronger, and could work longer before resting. The knife fitted his hand and obeyed his thought more truly. One or two cuts on his fingers had taught him caution. Many times Robin held the shorter piece of wood across the longer piece to see how it would look, and would ask, "Isn't it time now to put them together?" But each time Brother Luke's fingers sought out rough places that must be rubbed down with pumice.

Brother Luke was busy all day caring for the sick and the poor. From Vespers until the early bedtime he served his turn in the scriptorium, where all the writing was done.

Once, he had carried Robin to another part of the monastery, and showed him where records of everyday living were written and poems and psalteries copied. Each monk had a small enclosure of his own where he could be quiet to do his work.

Brother Luke set Robin down beside him on the oaken bench in his own particular place, where he could spread out the pages of handwritten manuscript on which he was working. The pages were of sheepskin, called parchment, and were covered with careful lettering and decorations. Gold leaf illumined the capitals and the delicate tracery which bordered the pages. Robin wished he had known how to read what he saw. He wished he could dip the quill into the inkpot and inscribe letters and draw pictures such as Brother Luke had done.

"Will you teach me to write?" asked Robin. "We were taught singing at the Brothers' School, but I know not writing. Will you teach me then?"

"Yes, my son, truly I will, when there are not so many people to care for. But come, now, back to thy cot. First, we shall stop to say a prayer in the chapel for thy strengthening."

He lifted Robin to his back again and started down the corridor.

In some places the passages were so crowded it was difficult to get through without stepping on someone. Old men and women in pitiful rags sat hunched against the wall or lay upon pallets. Among them went the Brothers of the order, and sisters from the priory near by, cleansing and feeding, dressing and comforting them. Ill-clad children ran about, and a small girl child clung to Brother Luke and begged to be carried.

A boy, not much older than Robin, came hobbling toward them on crutches. He smacked Robin as he passed and saluted him, seeing how Robin's legs were lame, even as his own.

"Good eve, Brother Crookshanks!" he cried, laughing as if it had been a great joke to be lame. "I see I have good company."

Robin's anger rose at the familiarity.

"Keep your filthy hands off me, lout!" he shouted. "Hound's meat! I am no more crook-shanked than you!" But even as he spoke Robin was considering the crutches, and thinking how convenient they would be for himself. Then he remembered that even yet his legs would not support him for a moment.

Brother Luke scolded the boy, but laughed, too, at Robin's anger.

"Fie on thee for an impertinent lad! Still, 'Crookshanks' he is, truly. His legs will be as good as thine one day, boy, and then he shall keep thee company right enough, on his feet." He went on toward the chapel, speaking to Robin over his shoulder as they went.

"The lad meant no offense when he called thee 'Crookshanks,' Master Robin. Tis but the way we all are named; for some oddity we have, or for where we live, or for what we do. This boy is called Geoffrey Atte-Water, because he lives by the River Fleet and tends the conduit there with his father. He was so called before he limped as he does now."

"Oh," said Robin, "I wondered why he is not called Geoffrey Crookshanks. Now I understand."

Brother Luke went on to speak of other names and how they began.

"Now I was called Chaucer, because my father was a shoemaker, but since I have taken a vow to be a monk, and to serve our Lord wherever I am most needed, I have taken the name of Luke, the physician in the Gospel."

"And my father is Sir John de Bureford because he came from that place. Is that the way of it?" asked Robin.

"That is the right of it," agreed the friar. "When Geoffrey called thee 'Crookshanks,' he did it because thy legs are *thy* legs and none others. Richard Smaltrot is he with the short step, and not Richard Crowfoot, whose feet splay out like fans."

Robin laughed.

They went into the chapel. It was empty, being between times for service.

Brother Luke placed Robin on the stone seat bordering the wall, propping him against the column which rose high to the vaulted roof.

"Say there thy prayers," he directed, "and in thy mind know thou'rt on thy knees. Forget not to be thankful for all thou hast. Remember thy lady mother and Sir John, thy father, who is at the wars, and pray for us all."

Then he left Robin and went apart to his own devotions. "But what have I to be thankful for?" Robin thought rebelliously. "How will my father like a son who is called 'Crookshanks'?" But somehow as he began his prayers he felt better.

As the days grew warmer, the plague abated somewhat. Fewer people came to the hospital for care, and those who had not died became well and went to their homes. The cloisters were once more free of strangers and the corridors cleared of beds and pallets.

Early one bright morning Brother Luke came for Robin, taking him on his back as before.

"See that thy hold is strong," he said, "for I shall carry thee a good way. 'Tis good exercise for thine arms to make thee hold on, and will be good exercise for me, too, carrying a great lad of ten."

Robin laughed, because he knew that he was small for his age.

"I have somewhat in mind for thee," said Brother Luke.

He carried Robin in and out of halls and chambers, kitchen and parlor, cloisters and outer court; through refectory and almonry, stopping, as always, in the chapel to say a prayer.

Then they went to the gardens at the far side of the monastery.

"Here thy whittling will be more at home," said the friar, settling Robin in a small trundle cart and giving him the pieces of the little cross which was almost finished.

"Brother Michael will welcome thee to his part of

the garden when thou'rt weary of being here. Brother Matthew will look out for thee, and yonder is Brother David, the stone mason. Wilt look after Robin?" he called to the monk in the carpenter shop.

Brother Matthew nodded and left his work to examine what Robin was doing.

"Fret not," he said. "I see he is one of us."

" 'Twill be a cross when 'tis done," said Robin in greeting, putting the two pieces together to show how they went. "But how to fasten them I know not. Could you tell me?"

"I will, surely," the monk assured him. "But I have better tools. Come nearer where we can reach them." He moved the trundle cart close to the workbench, where he found a chisel.

"Now we shall make a half joint, so, and fit it tightly, cutting each piece only halfway through the wood, so the crosspiece will just fit into the upright one." He showed Robin how to hold the sharp tool and how carefully he must work so that it wouldn't go through the wood entirely.

"Then," he explained, "we shall secure it with fish glue, and the dust which comes from using the rubbing stone to polish the wood will fill in the least crack and make all smooth."

He went back to his work.

Robin, too, went to work. It was exciting to use the sharp chisel. It slid easily into the wood, peeling off the smallest slivers which fell in a pleasant litter around him. Soon the square place appeared where the other piece of wood should fit. For some reason he did not know Robin felt very content. He loved the smell of the wood he was whittling, even the acrid smell of the oak that Brother Matthew was working. He liked the sharp whistle of the plane as it slid over the board, and the ringing sound of the chisel on stone from the mason's shed. Even the tiresome call of the cuckoo in the walnut tree was only a pleasant sound of summer. The sky above was like the garment of Our Lady: blue, gold-bordered.

Robin stopped to rest, watching the birds that darted about the garden.

He felt so strong that he was sure he soon would be able to get up and walk. He began to whistle, and set to work again.

For a long time only these homely sounds were heard in the garden close, for the monks did not talk at their work.

Then it happened. The sharp chisel slipped and cut a gash across the longer piece of the cross. It broke.

Away flew the other piece as far as Robin could throw it, and after it went the chisel, narrowly missing Brother Matthew's head. Robin's face was drawn into a black cloud of anger, and if he had been able, he would have stormed out of the garden. But he was bound to stay where he was, so he took out his anger in words.

"Treacherous misguided tool!" he shouted. "I'll have no more of you!"

Brother Matthew looked up in astonishment. " 'Tis not the tool that is at fault, but thine unskilled hands," he said quietly.

"If thou'rt to learn to use it, patience and care are better teachers than a bad temper."

"Think you I am but a carpenter's son and apprentice?"

But as Brother Matthew kept his steady gaze on Robin, anger evaporated. He covered his eyes with his arms and wished he had been truly a carpenter's son. Then his father would not have been away at the wars, or his mother in waiting upon the Queen. They would have been at home, and he with them.

"Tomorrow is another day," comforted Brother Matthew. "Take thy rest for now, and thou wilt do better work next time. Here is Brother Luke coming to care for thee. I shall not tell him how nearly I lost my head." Brother Matthew's eyes twinkled as he reassured Robin, who had given him a questioning look.

Later, while the good friar cared for him, rubbing his legs and back, working the muscles of his hands and arms, he said, "I was tired, but now I feel better. You are very kind."

"I see thou'rt getting stronger. It may be that this rubbing helps thee. How, I know not. I am no physician; I am but a foolish friar. But it may stir up thy blood and make thee more comfortable. God's good time, His sunshine, and the love that is borne thee are all healing. A bright spirit helps, too, and that thou hast."

"Today in the garden I felt that soon I should walk," said Robin. "I must get well before my father returns from the wars."

"Whether thou'lt walk soon I know not. This I know. We must teach thy hands to be skillful in many ways, and we must teach thy mind to go about whether thy legs will carry thee or no. For reading is another door in the wall, dost understand, my son?"

Robin smiled and nodded. "Yes," he said. "I see now what you mean by the door in the wall."

"We shall read together. Then there is somewhat of the earth and stars that Brother Hubert can tell thee: how they go in their seasons so that in summer when we rise for the midnight office Orion is here. Yet in winter, at the same hour, he is over there." Brother Luke stopped rubbing to point in different directions overhead as he went on.

"Some say that the earth extendeth just so far, then

droppeth off into a vast sea. Perhaps it is so, I know not. But if it be so, how come the stars out again in their season? Who knows? Not I. But someday we shall know all."

"Will you teach me to write, too, and how to make letters as you promised?" Robin asked. "It sounds exciting now, to learn, and I wish to send a letter to my father."

"We shall begin today. We shall divide the days into teaching thy mind and teaching thy hands, then weariness shall not give thee excuse for discouragement." Then Robin knew that Brother Luke had seen him throw the pieces of the cross and the chisel. Yet the friar neither spoke of it nor showed in any way that he was disappointed.

"Rest while I am gone," continued Brother Luke, "and I shall bring quill and parchment to pen a letter for thee. It so happens that a hundred men at arms and a hundred foot soldiers have sworn to serve loyally their King and the city of London and are leaving for the Scottish border tomorrow. With them goes a minstrel well known to us, one John-go-in-the-Wynd. He will gladly carry thy letter and put it into thy father's hands."

He soon returned with pen, inkpot, and parchment, and arranged them on the desk near Robin.

"Say this," Robin began, then went on to dictate the words as the monk penned them.

Sir John de Bureford
from his son Robin—Greeting

It is a fine thing that your son Robin is left to the care of strangers. Had it not been for Brother Luke, who is writing this letter, I should be dead. As you know, my lady mother had been commanded to attendance on the Queen at Windsor, and I was left to await the coming of John-the-Fletcher in the care of Dame Ellen.

Just before the Feast of St. Matthew, the twenty-fourth of February, I woke one morning unable to rise from my bed, being very ill. So that when John-the-Fletcher came to take me to my Lord Peter de Lindsay's castle in Shropshire, I was unable to go. Wherefore he sent a physician to care for me, who came not again, but left me as before in Dame Ellen's care. The men at arms are with you, as well you know. The house servants, even old Gregory, have left our service, for the plague had them. Ellen, too, was taken of it, and I was left alone and helpless. My legs are as useless as two sausages. Bent ones.

Now I am in the care of this good Brother at St. Mark's. How, then, shall I do? Send me a letter, I beg you, and Farewell.

"Now, attend," said Brother Luke. "I shall read this slowly, pointing out each letter and word, so this may be thy first lesson." The two heads bent over the parchment together, Brother Luke's tonsured, Robin's dark and thickly thatched.

"Oh," said Robin, "you have made it look like poetry with red capitals!"

"Yes," agreed Brother Luke, "but when it is read to thee, 'twill not sound like poetry, I'll vow. Thou hast not minced words in thy letter."

Slowly and carefully he spelled out the letter to Robin, who would not change a word of it, but signed his name with Brother Luke guiding his hand. The friar folded it and took it to the scriptorium to seal before sending it off, then gave it to John-go-in-the-Wynd, who waited.

JUNE passed, and the days lengthened into summer. The plague had died out, but with its going went many of the people of London, even some of the monks. Once more the monastery kept its usual round of service to God and humanity. The monks who were left added to their own the duties of those who had died. Brother Luke sometimes helped in the preparation of food. Sometimes he carried Robin down into the kitchen, where he could be warm on a wet day. It was there that he finished the little cross.

"Although it is yet too soon for thee to carve figures for choir stalls or for bosses for chapel, a child's puppet could be made more easily. Why not make one for that poor girl child who hung to my skirts that day? She dwelleth by Houndsditch in a poor hovel where I go on my errands."

"A girl's plaything?" asked Robin. Then he began to think what fun it might be to carve out a face. He might even make the arms and legs so they would move. "Yes," he said. "I will try."

So began the making of the doll for the little girl. Head and body were to be in one piece, with arms and legs jointed.

"Brother Matthew will help thee to work that out," said Brother Luke.

Soft pine again was used, because it was easier to cut.

Robin became so excited at seeing real features emerge from the piece of wood that he could hardly bear to take time to attend to his studies. Reading went well, and he was beginning to make fair characters in writing with the quill.

On clear nights Brother Hubert took him to a high tower of the monastery to tell him of the stars. He told Robin, too, of far countries: the Holy Land where crusaders had fought for the tomb of our Lord, and of Greece and Rome, whose ancient languages were the beginnings of many other tongues. He told of Roman legions who had come to Britain centuries before, and of Saxon and Danish kings who in turn had ruled their land. Robin couldn't always remember which ones came first, but he liked to hear Brother Hubert tell about them.

One day Robin was sitting in the trundle cart finishing the child's doll when Brother Luke came into the garden.

"Thy hands are well used to the chisel now," he said, in praise of Robin's work. "That is a face and body right enough, and I see thou'rt attaching the arms. Will they move then?"

"Yes," said Robin. "See how this peg fits into the shoulder then slips into the top of the arms, and it swings. See!"

"It will make a little child very happy," said the friar. "Now, because the day is so fine, and thou'rt getting so strong, it might be well if we should go fishing."

Fishing? Could he really leave the hospice and go fishing? Even the fun of fitting arms and legs to the doll could not keep Robin from wanting to get out into the fields and away from bench and bed, stool and trundle cart.

"I could sit against a tree and fish, too, think you?"

"No doubt," agreed Brother Luke. "Come, then." He

lifted Robin to his back and they went, down the green, to the brook outside the walls.

They fished for a time, each catching several trout, which they wrapped in leaves. The sun shone warm through the leafy grove. Insects droned in the noon heat, and the water slipped musically over green-mossed stones.

It was very still.

Suddenly the quiet was burst with the shout of boys' voices. Six or seven urchins ran over the green, stripping off clothing as they came. Robin, looking over his shoulder, saw Geoffrey Atte-Water, the same lad he had first seen limping through the corridors of St. Mark's. Geoffrey raced down the bank ahead of all the rest, swinging his crutches ahead of him and taking in his stride twice as much ground as the other boys.

Geoffrey saw Robin at the same moment.

"Hi! Crookshanks!" he called. "Art finding fish for thy fasting?"

Off came the last ragged garment, down went the crutches, and with a "Whoosh!" he was into the water with the others and away with the current. Thrashing arms and legs beat the water into foam and spoiled the fishing.

Robin wished with all his heart that he could go into the water and swim, too. It was all very well for Brother Luke to bring him fishing, but it only seemed to make it harder that he couldn't run about or swim like the other boys.

The friar saw Robin's hungry look.

"Off with thy jerkin," he said, at the same time rising and taking off his own habit. "We'll give thee a good bath and cleanse thy humor. Who knows? Mayhap we can teach thee to swim!" He pulled off Robin's hosen and carried him into the water, holding and dipping him where the current ran deep.

"Now swing thy arms about, with fingers closed to push the water back."

Robin pushed, and felt himself moving along with Brother Luke walking and supporting him. All the troubles of the past months seemed to float away with the running of the brook and strength and power to flow into his arms.

It was wonderful.

Brother Luke didn't allow him to stay long in the water, but promised to bring him every day.

"For some time I have had this in mind," he said. "Now I know I was right. This will make thine arms even stronger, and soon they will help thee to get about on land as well."

"How?" asked Robin. But even as he said it, he knew what Brother Luke meant. Crutches! That was it! With crutches he would be able to go about as Geoffrey did. He could play at duck on a rock with the boys. He could join them in hoodman-blind or hide-and-seek. Crutches would be almost as much fun as stilts!

Then Robin remembered that his father expected him to be a knight. How could he ride horseback in chain mail while his legs were bent and he had to use crutches?

How could he face his father? How bear his mother's pitying look? How would they feel to have a son who could not fulfill his knightly duties?

"I see thou hast my meaning," said the friar, as he finished dressing Robin. "Crutches or crosses as thou'lt have it. 'Tis all the same thing. Remember, even thy crutches can be a door in a wall. By the time they are made, thou'lt be ready for them, God willing. Up, now, and hold fast whilst we go up the hill."

From that day forward swimming became a part of Robin's everyday life. Besides reading, writing, and the study of history and the stars Robin was given certain duties in the routine of the church. At the lectern during rehearsals he turned the pages of the missal, a book of music notes large enough for all the Brothers to see as they stood in the chantry. Each day, too, he worked with Brother Matthew in the carpentry shop. He liked the music and the carpentry better than the reading and writing, but best of all he liked the swimming. It made him feel free and powerful.

Even on cloudy or rainy days, and when the weather was quite cool, Robin was taken for his daily swim, and soon he was able to dive beneath the water and play tricks on the good friar. Once, when the boys saw Robin's little boat, they begged to be allowed to sail it, too. But they were all so eager to try it that soon its rigging was broken and its pennant dragging. So Robin helped each of them make a boat of his own. Geoffrey's was made from a piece of the willow overhanging the brook. A twig stuck into a wormhole made the mast and another twig through a leaf served for a sail. Then Dickon must have one, then Alfred, and the swimming hole became a boatyard.

Sometimes they marked out squares on the sandy bank and played a game of checkers with round stones. Some-

times, on hot days, all the time was spent in the water, and the boys raced Robin to the weir and back. Once Robin beat them all.

"Crookshanks, here, is as fast as any of us," Geoffrey said proudly. Then Robin felt as if he were one of them.

Once, when Robin dived under water and hid in the rushes, Brother Luke at first scolded him, for he was frightened. Then he said, "But I am glad for thy mischief, for it is a sign thou'rt well."

Robin had another reason for knowing he was well, but he kept it secret.

Work was begun on the crutches.

They were to be simple, straight staves with crosspieces at the top to fit under Robin's arms.

Brother Matthew had found the wood of proper kind and size, then he sawed it the right length, allowing a little for finishing. Brother Luke wheeled Robin to the shed where he could watch. When the first piece of wood was put into the vise and Brother Matthew began to draw the spoke shave down the length of it, Robin thought it time to tell his secret, for he wanted very much to have a hand in making the crutches with which he hoped to walk.

"Can I shape the pieces, think you?" he asked. "Look!" he directed. "I can bear my weight upon my feet, though I cannot stand long alone, nor can I straighten. But can I not lean upon the bench?"

To the surprise of both Brothers, Robin hitched along slowly toward Brother Matthew's workbench, where he leaned for a few moments before he found it necessary to sit down.

"Now praise our Lord's mercy!" said Brother Luke fervently, at the same time putting forth a high stool for Robin to sit on. "Now 'twill be thine own crutches thou wilt wear made by thine own hands." Brother Matthew blessed himself to show how grateful he was, and arranged the work so that Robin could better attend to it for himself.

It was more exciting to work at a real bench, to draw the sharp knife along the clean wood; to hear it "snick" as the knife took hold, then slither off into shavings. The oak was very hard, and took real strength to work, but swimming had given Robin good muscle in his arms, so that little by little he was able to shape the staff.

Several weeks went by before Robin finished the crutches. But at last they were done, and he could hardly wait to try them.

"There should be padding and leather on the crosspieces," said Brother Luke. "Let us go into the city to the Pouchmakers' Guild. I have errands for the Prior as well. Besides, it is Midsummer Eve! We shall see the gaiety."

"Shall I walk then?" asked Robin. "For look you, I have been trying the crutches already and can go at a good pace. See you?" Robin slid off the stool, fitted the crutches under his arms, and was off across the Garth all in one motion.

"Softly, softly," Brother Luke advised. " 'Tis a good way into the city, even though its sounds and odors do seem to reach us here. It would be better to go pickaback and carry thy crosses most of the way. Thou'lt be glad of my old back ere we come to Ludgate, I'll be bound."

It was exciting to go back into the city, especially this Midsummer Eve. The doorways were decked with branches of green birch, long fennel, and St.-John's-wort. Some had garlands of flowers—white lilies and such like. Neighbor was merry with neighbor, and those who had wealth set out food and drink before their houses for all who passed by.

"Can we not stay even a little while?" Robin begged.

"No, my son, when we have done our errands, we shall go back."

The Bracegirdler down Leather Lane willingly gave Robin enough leather to cover the crosspieces of the crutches and hair to stuff it.

" 'Tis not fit to be sold," he said, "being poorly dyed. But 'twill serve thy purpose."

They were not far from Robin's home, but he had no wish to see it empty and deserted. How he wished it had been open, and his father and mother there!

ONE Friday toward the end of September the monks of the choir stood practicing in the chantry. Standing by the lectern to turn the pages of the missal was Robin in scarlet cassock and white linen cotta. They were singing the Sanctus, and had just come to the Amen when the verger appeared.

He held up his hand for their attention.

"A messenger has come for young Robin from his father," he said. "Let him come with me." Robin followed the verger down the corridor to the parlor, the thud of his crutches alternating with the sound of his soft shoes on the stone floor. Robin wondered who the messenger could be, Elfred the Dane or Rolfe the Bowyer? It was neither. It was John-go-in-the-Wynd, the minstrel, who had carried Robin's letter to his father weeks ago.

"Good young master," he said to Robin, "this letter I bring from thy noble father in all haste. For long I could not find him, for that the battle did go first to one place then to another. And the Scots be so fierce in fighting that often the battle went against our side."

"And how goes it now?" asked Robin. "Is my father alive? Is he well and safe?"

"It goes well now," said John. "And here is thy letter."

"My thanks, John-go-in-the-Wynd," said Robin, then

to God
on high.
And on
Earth

he took the letter to the light to read it. His hands shook, for it was the first word he had had from his father since early winter, the first letter he had ever received indeed, and it was exciting to know that now he could read it for himself.

Robin, son of John de Bureford,
from his father—Greeting

It grieves me, my son, more than I can tell you to know that you are ill. I thank Heaven it is not the Plague you have had, for that enemy has slain more men than battle, besides the women and children it has taken toll of. It shocked me to learn that you had been left to the care of strangers. Your mother would hardly bear it if I should tell her, but I will not. She is with the Queen, who is in delicate health. I dare not say where, lest this letter fall into unfriendly hands.

She supposes that you are far away from London, in Shropshire. It is well. Let her continue to think so, for in truth you soon will be, God willing and your health permitting, for I have requested the Prior to arrange your journey with all speed. You will travel in care of Brother Luke and John-go-in-the-Wynd.

I had a message from Sir Peter only the day before your letter reached me asking what had happened to you, for John-the-Fletcher never returned. Some evil befell him surely, for he was an honorable servant. Sir Peter was wounded while bringing up forces to my aid, so sorely wounded that he has been taken to a castle near by where he will stay until he is able to be taken home.

The Scots are being slowly pushed back and we are gaining ground, since receiving the added help from London and the nearby towns. The King hopes for a peace by the Sacrament of Christmas, but the Scots are a stubborn race.

I trust that you are improving in health, my son, and in God's Grace.

So, Farewell,

Your father,
Sir John de Bureford
Thursday after the Feast
of John the Baptist

Preparations for Robin's departure began immediately. Brother Luke and Brother Matthew between them devised a sort of chair-saddle in which Robin could ride. Part of it was to be made of iron, then it was to be finished with padding and leather at the saddler's. They made another journey in to town, taking to Dame Agnes such of Robin's clothing as needed repair. The ironmonger promised to send the framework to the saddler by the following Monday, as early as he was able. The saddler agreed to have his part of the work done by evening of the next day. Dame Agnes put aside her embroidery to do what was required of her, and she, too, promised that the work would be finished early in the week.

Meantime, John-go-in-the-Wynd helped Brother Luke lay out a plan of travel. Brother Andrew took Brother Luke's place as cook's helper, and the Prior gave orders for certain foods to be put aside for the journey.

When all was ready, saddlebags were filled with clothing on one side and food on the other. There were loaves fresh from the oven, a great slab of bacon, cheese, some dried herring, fruits from the garden, and, last of all, a pasty was set in the top. In it were larks and a rabbit seasoned with herbs and colored yellow with saffron. The fruits were apples and early pears and plums which Brother Michael had picked from the trees and vines kept trained flat along the garden wall.

" 'Twill be good for noon quench," he said, "when there is no ale to be had, and will mind thee to be thankful for God's gifts."

On the morning they set out the air was crisp and cool. The sun had not risen above the horizon, but it cast a bright glow into the heavens, promising a fair day. Larks rose from the meadow, straight up, as if from pure joy, and they sang,

Robin thought, as if it had been the first day of the world. He felt sorry to leave Brother Matthew and all the others who had been so good to him, but it was exciting to start out on the long journey.

"There are over a hundred English miles to go," said John-go-in-the-Wynd, "and frost is not far off, so we must go steadily."

He and Brother Luke shared Bayard, the horse, taking turn about, one riding, the other walking beside Robin.

They went toward the Oxford Road, then turned westward through Holborn, stopping a moment to pray at each wayside cross, just as if they had been on a pilgrimage.

"It is indeed a sort of pilgrimage," said Brother Luke, "for always we shall set forth for the honor of God and in the hope that young Robin will be even stronger at the end of our journey than he is now."

Because it was a market day, the road was crowded with people and animals going toward London. For long no one had been allowed to come into the city because of the plague, but now that the danger was over, people came from everywhere to exchange goods. Some rode in carts piled high with produce: cabbages and bags of grain, cheese, butter and bacon, chickens and ducks. Some drove flocks of goats and sheep, or led pigs or carried faggots of firewood.

By noon the promise of sunshine failed and the travelers took refuge from a sudden shower under a spreading beech. They were joined by a minstrel, who was glad to share their bread and cheese and pay for his entertainment by singing a lay which John-go-in-the-Wynd picked out on the harp.

"Brother Michael's pears and grapes are a welcome treat to my thirsty throat," said John.

"It seems a week since we broke our fast this morning," said Robin, eating hungrily.

"We've come a goodly way since early morning," said John. "But we must not linger or we shall not reach the White Swan by nightfall. I have it from Peter the Hayward that it lies but a good day's journey out of London. It is well to be safe housed after dark, for cutpurses and roisterers do roam the country hereabout."

"If my father were with us, we should have no fear of anyone," said Robin.

"We shall have faith in the Father of us all," said the friar.

It was Brother Luke's turn to ride, so John-go-in-the-Wynd walked beside Robin. As he strode along, he began to sing, playing the tune on his harp. The tune was lively and well measured. Bayard stepped up his pace, the jennet pranced and arched her neck, and Robin wanted to get down and swing along with the others.

"Lend me a hand, John-go-in-the-Wynd, and set the crutches so I may walk awhile," he directed, interrupting the song. Brother Luke looked back to see what was delaying them, but nodded as he saw Robin afoot, and John again plucking the strings of the little harp. They hummed as if they had been voices, so that Robin's fingers itched to touch them.

He watched John's fingers as they searched out the tune, how they danced on the strings to make the differing chords. He noticed the smooth wood of the harp and how the strings were held with wooden pegs. He wished he could play on it, and wondered if he could make such an instrument.

Now that noon was past, there were few people on the road, but soon they fell in with a peasant with a shepherd's crook over his shoulder. They asked the way to the next village.

"The village lies just yonder about an hour's journey,"

he said. "The road goes through the wood, over the downs, crosses a bridge, then winds up the hill where thou'lt find a butter cross where the market is held. Likely there'll be nought to buy there, as 'tis past noon. Beyond the cross the road turns more northerly and there is a fork where it divides. Beyond that I know not how it goes."

"Go you to the village?" asked Robin.

"No, I go to the forest of my lord's manor where wood for house fires may be gathered. We country folk may have such branches as can be gathered by hook or by crook from the standing trees of the lord's forest." He left them with a "good day" and crossed the field.

Robin grew tired, for he had walked more than a mile. John-go-in-the-Wynd helped him into the saddle again and fastened the crutches on behind.

A windmill swung its giant arms in slow obedience to the wind and a farmer passed them carrying a sack of grain to be ground. Over the treetops the spire of the village church could be seen, and thatched cottages began to appear at the road's edge.

They entered the village where the stone bridge crossed a stream. The butter cross in the center square stood open to the four winds. The stone paving was still wet from the washing down after market, and the last of the farmers gathered baskets and gear before going home.

Brother Luke was ahead, still riding Bayard the horse, but here he stopped and changed places with John-go-in-the-Wynd.

The road continued to rise beyond the village, winding between hedgerows of hawthorn now starred with rosy fruit.

Robin drew his cloak around him, for the air was damp and chilly.

About a mile beyond the village, at the top of the hill,

they came to the fork in the road. Another cross to the memory of Queen Eleanor stood at the dividing point, but no signpost.

"Now, by my faith," declared John-go-in-the-Wynd, "I know not which road to take." He drew rein and waited for Brother Luke to come abreast of him.

"Nor do I," said the friar, "never having traveled this way."

"Did he not say the right fork?" asked Robin.

"The fellow said not which road leadeth to Oxford," said John, "but I am for the right fork."

"My memory serves me ill," said the friar. "Whether he said one or the other I know not. Let us say the office here at the cross before we go on. Then we shall go to the right. But it may be that we shall not find the White Swan and shall have to sleep in a hedgerow."

By the time they started on their way again the wind blew hard and spits of rain warned them of more to follow. Brother Luke drew his cowl over his head and unfolded a furred robe from the pack to put around Robin. For several miles they plodded on without speaking. The rain held off, but dark clouds scudded low, and the wind was searching.

A lonely peasant cottage stood back from the road, but as yet there was no sign of the White Swan. Robin grew very tired and wished the day's journey had come to an end.

"Will it be soon, think you?" he asked, not wishing to say how his back ached.

"Whether it be soon or late, I know not," answered the friar. "But these old legs need rest." Then he shouted to John-go-in-the-Wynd, who was some distance ahead.

"What sayest thou, John? How goeth it? Are we near to the inn?" John shook his head and shouted back, turning

Bayard and waiting for the others to come up.

"We must have taken the wrong fork," he said. "I see no inn, and night is nigh. Ahead lies a dark forest, and see 'tis raining now. Shall we seek shelter here by the road?"

"It is an ill thing for young Robin to sleep out in the damp, but if such be our fortune, then we must make the best of it."

"Shall we sleep on the ground?" asked Robin. "What a lark! I have never yet in my life slept out of doors, though it may as well have been out of doors when the east wind blew through the wind hole."

"We might go on to the forest and be more sheltered from wind and rain," offered John-go-in-the-Wynd, "but that wild beasts do roam about and highwaymen lurk in the edge of it to leap out at passersby. I'm for staying here. I have flint and steel to make a fire." He dismounted and led Bayard to the edge of the road where he could examine the lay of the land.

Said Brother Luke, " 'Tis nought for me to sleep in Mother Nature's arms. Many a night have I been grateful for the comfort of solid ground. And mayhap we can cover young Robin to keep him dry." He followed John to the field's edge.

"Why, here 'tis! The very thing!" he cried. "An ancient tree trunk fallen from age and hollowed with dry rot. It hath stood enough years to make it both wide and deep. We shall not be ill-found after all. Come, young master, let me help thee, for I know thou'rt galled by the saddle, be it ever so soft." He helped Robin to get down from Jenny's back and adjusted the crutches under his arms.

"It is good that the fullers do shrink and pound this cloth, for it is well-nigh rainproof," the friar went on as he bustled about getting the saddlebags down, putting the furred rug inside the great log, and leading Jenny to be tethered to the thicket.

John-go-in-the-Wynd tied Bayard beside her, leaving them both on a loose rein so they might crop the grass.

Robin stood with his back to the wind, holding his cloak about him. This was a real adventure. Even though he might never be a knight in armor and go to battle to defend England, he would know what it was like to make his bed on God's earth, feel the prick of rain in his face, and instead of brocaded bed curtains, see dark clouds making a canopy over him.

John cleared a space shielded from the rain on the far side of the log where the ground was still dry, then set it about with stones, and searched for dry twigs to make his fire. Farther down the sloping meadow he found a ruined ox yoke left by a careless peasant which would burn long and well. A few dry leaves and some of the punky rotted wood served as tinder when steel and flint struck a spark in the shelter of the hollow log; and soon there was a cheerful fire which drove back the night and storm. They roasted apples in the fire, but ate the pasty cold, and hunger sauced it better than the finest cook could have done.

WHEN Robin woke next morning John-go-in-the-Wynd had a good fire going, even though rain fell at intervals and the wind was still blowing. He was grilling slices of bacon over the fire, and standing beside him was Brother Luke holding a large loaf from which he was cutting huge slices of bread. He heard Robin stirring and greeted him with his blessing.

"I hope thy log house kept thee dry," he said.

"John has been inquiring of the shepherd yonder about the White Swan. He says we are beyond it and it is over on the other road."

"I should have remembered," said John. "But it is long since I came this way. We truly took the wrong turning."

"Let it be a lesson for us," said the good friar. "We mind how the two roads were one where we stopped at the Eleanor cross. Yet so swiftly did the two forks divide that now we are several miles from the one we should have taken. So it goeth. God grant we may never be worse off than now when we take the wrong turning."

Not far beyond the place where they had camped a path led through the wood. There they were somewhat sheltered from wind and rain. The shepherd had said to follow the path to a certain stream at the far side of the wood which would shortly lead them to the highroad. They found it without difficulty. John-go-in-the-Wynd sang so heartily and made such music with the harp that the way seemed short.

When they reached the stream, Brother Luke said, " 'Tis best for thee to go into the water as always, so off with thy clothes, Master Robin."

"But it is cold, and flesh creeps at the thought of it," said Robin, shivering.

"Come, my son. Doth thy father stop to say 'I cannot go into battle for my King because arrows are sharp'? Off with thy clothes, I say, else thou'lt lose the strength and skill thou hast begun to have. 'Tis a long way from freezing." While he spoke he lifted Robin down and helped him to undress and go into the river.

At first Robin's teeth chattered, but in a few moments he was warmer and glad he had made the effort.

At noon the little company stopped at the sign of the Shepherd's Bush for ale to go with their bread and cheese.

The host sat himself down beside the friar and asked how things went in London.

"Travelers from London be few since the plague," he said. "Thinkest thou the plague is over?"

" 'Tis quiet, at least," answered Brother Luke. "And we believe 'tis gone."

"And how go the wars? Be they going well? Hast heard how 'tis with my lord the King?"

"It goes hardly, but it goes our way," said Robin importantly. "I have had a letter saying that the King hopes for a peace by the Feast of Christmas."

"*Peace*?" said the host wonderingly. "Peace is what we all hope for. But we find it seldom. For if 'tis not the Welsh 'tis the Scots. If 'tis neither one nor the other, then 'tis neighbor against neighbor, or 'tis the lord of the manor against the peasants, begging thy pardon, young master."

They set out again, and made good speed, reaching the village of Heathcot by dusk. There they found an inn at the edge of town, its thatch pulled down over its eyes of windows wherein could be seen a smoky light from the fire.

A creaking sign showed the picture of the White Hart.

"An innocent name," said the friar. "But this place hath a fearsome look."

John-go-in-the-Wynd held horse and jennet while the friar went in to inquire about lodging for themselves and their tired beasts.

When he came out, he said, "I have a doubt whether this be a good place to stay. There are ill-seeming ruffians sitting about the fire, and the goodwife hath a slatternly look, but we have no choice. Come, then." He helped Robin to the ground and got him in to the fire, for he was cold and stiff from the long day in the saddle. John took the horse and jennet to the stable, a tumbledown affair at the back.

It was fortunate that there was food in the saddlebags, for the White Hart had none to offer. Leather noggins of ale were all that could be had, and when Brother Luke paid for it and for the room Robin saw the two strangers fasten their look on the money pouch Brother Luke carried for their journey.

He wished they could have slept out of doors, as they had done the night before. But he was chilled, and the fire felt good even though it smoked and made his eyes smart.

As soon as they had eaten the bread and cheese, Brother Luke helped Robin up the narrow stair and put him to bed on the straw pallet.

Brother Luke fell asleep as soon as he lay down. John was soon snoring, too. Robin could hear the wood in the door vibrate with the sound, for John lay just outside the room, to guard it.

Robin was so tired he felt as if every bone pushed through the straw to find the unyielding boards beneath him. He slept and woke, slept and woke, till it seemed as if it should be morning. The two evil-looking men still muttered below over their ale, getting louder as it grew later.

At first Robin didn't notice what they were saying. Then something like "the minstrel's hefty look" caught his ear, so he held his breath to listen, then heard one of them say,

"Come midnight, when 'tis darkest, I shall take yon minstrel, and thou the friar. Be sure to get the leather bag safe. The child will be nothing, for he cannot move fast, and he will sleep sound. He was like to die of weariness while he ate. Hark! The big one snores like a braying jack!"

They were planning to steal the money pouch. What should he do? He must do something and do it quickly. How could he wake the weary friar without noise? Or how warn John-go-in-the-Wynd without opening the door? Which

should he do first? Perhaps it would be better if he woke the friar first.

Softly, softly, Robin slid off the pallet, trying not to rustle the straw. He hitched himself along the floor, but the sound of his moving over the boards alarmed the two who were talking below.

"Hisst!" said the big one, for Robin knew it was he.

"What is that?"

They were still for a moment. So was Robin.

" 'Tis nought," answered the other scornfully. "Thou'rt easily frighted for so great a bully. 'Tis but a scurrying rat. 'Tis nigh the mid of night," he went on, "for I heard a cock crowing. Shall we start then?"

"Wait," said the first voice. "Because they are city folk, the cock's crow might wake them. So wait a little."

Robin dared not move, yet there was no time to lose. He reached out his hand, but it fell short of touching the friar's frock by almost a foot. He lifted himself as high as he could on his hands, moved one, bearing his weight, slid both legs after slowly, slowly then moved the other hand, and slid forward again. It did make some sound, but when he listened he heard only the sputter of the fire and a hound's far-off barking. Perhaps the ale had silenced the louts.

He touched the friar's shoulder. Brother Luke, used to waking at midnight for Matins, sat up immediately, saw the blur of white that was Robin's face, but said nothing, only looked steadily into Robin's eyes until his own grew used to the dark.

Robin whispered in his ear.

"Robbers," he said. "Thieves!" pointing downward. Brother Luke nodded, held his fingers to his lips, and rose to his feet without a sound. He crept to the door, keeping close to the wall so as not to tread on a squeaky board. He lifted the latch slowly and opened the door inch by inch, so that John, who lay against it, rolled into the room, still snoring.

Brother Luke took firm hold of John's shoulder, and at the same time touched his mouth with a finger to warn him not to speak. John was awake in the middle of a snore, but he, too, was used to being wakened suddenly, and was well acquainted with danger, so, knowing that he always snored in his sleep, he began to snore again, nodding his head the while to show that he knew what was afoot. He gave one great snore, sighed heavily, then moaned, as if he had been dreaming and had turned over. He used that time to get soundlessly to his feet.

Luckily he had brought cloaks and other gear in the saddlebags. His own cloak, which was travel worn and patched, he presently tied by a corner to an iron-bound chest which stood under the window. He motioned for Brother Luke to go down first, showing by gestures how he would hand down the bags, Robin's crutches, and lastly Robin. Then he would follow. It was not far to the ground, for the inn was only a cottage.

Would Robin be able to hold his weight by his arms? He could only try. It was a tight squeeze for the friar to go through the small window, but he got through and by way of the cloak, down to the ground. He grunted when the saddlebags landed against his stomach but was ready to reach up for the crutches when John leaned out to hand them down.

Then came Robin. John pulled the cloak in and wrapped it partly around him so that he could get out of the window without falling, and held him under the arms until he could get hold of the cloak. Robin was able to let himself down slowly hand over hand to land safely beside the waiting friar. Suddenly great scuffling and shouting began. John scrambled out of the window and slid to the ground.

Then Robin heard the big fellow say, "By my beard, the birds have flown!"

"The night hag take thee!" shouted the other. "We stayed too long over the ale!"

"Run!" shouted John catching up the saddlebags, while the friar hoisted Robin to his back, giving him the crutches to hold.

They ran, but already the thieves were sliding down the cloak and at their heels.

Robin turned and with one hand thrust the crutches between the big fellow's feet, throwing him to the ground and bringing the other ruffian down on top of him.

"Haste!" urged Robin. "They are so befuddled that each is pounding the other, thinking it is us they have caught."

They got to the stables, mounted the horses, and were away before the two oafs had untangled themselves. Brother Luke took Robin with him on Bayard, and John-go-in-the-Wynd, carrying the saddlebags, rode on Jenny.

Not until they were well through the village and out into the open country did they stop to rest and consider what they should do. There, just off the highroad, stood a great barn. The door was secured by a padlock, but John-go-in-the-Wynd managed to get in through the granary window. He opened one of the smaller doors to the weary travelers and there they finished the short night.

Before leaving in the early morning the friar said,

"We must leave a farthing for our host, whoever he may be, and our blessing." So saying, he said the morning office before they set out again.

THE next morning the weather cleared, and by the end of the fourth day the spires of Oxford appeared. Before long they crossed the Cherwell into the High Street. Everywhere Robin looked, there were students, walking about or talking on street corners. They filled the punts and barges that crowded the two rivers. They sprawled under the park trees eating bread and cheese, but wherever they were, they talked and talked and talked.

Most of the students were poor, and were dressed in every sort of particolored gown or tunic.

"It seems to me," said Robin, "as if they try to see how outlandish they can make themselves look."

The travelers went up the High then turned on past the Saxon Tower and the market cross to St. John's College, where they were received with courtesy and where they spent the night.

Beyond Oxford the country began to be more rolling.

Sometimes the road led through forests, then, again, it ran beside the river, crossed a bridge, and went up through a village. Once they had to turn aside and allow a cavalcade of horsemen to pass. It swept by in a fine parade of shining mail, bright banners, and gaily caparisoned horses. In their midst rode a lady with her attendants. Robin wished the lady had been his mother.

Where was his mother now? Did she know about him and where he was? Did she know that he walked with the help of crutches?

They followed the cavalcade up the winding road to the top of the hill, where there was a sign announcing a fair at Wychwood Bec.

"There will be jousting!" said Robin.

"There will be dancing!" said John-go-in-the-Wynd.

"And there will be little praying," said Brother Luke. "There will be no room at the inn, so we must not linger long."

"Let us see a little of the fun," begged Robin.

So they turned aside and spent some hours at the fair, tethering the horses near the gate, giving a penny to a lad for watching them.

All the country people had come from miles around. They had brought cattle and sheep, dairy butter and cheese, whatever had been their portion after giving what was due to the lord of the manor.

Lombards from Europe were there with goods from far-off lands. There were silks and velvets from Italy and France, laces from Flanders.

Robin wanted to be everywhere at once. He wanted to watch the tournament, the bear baiting, the wrestling, and the racing. He wanted to taste all the food: the pigeon pies, the honey tarts, that suckling pig with the apple in its mouth, and the jugged hare. He flitted from one booth to the other with Brother Luke after him.

Finally Brother Luke said, "Hast seen enough, lad? It is a good way to the next hospice, they tell me, and we have two or three days' journey ahead of us. So come, my son."

"Let me see only the rest of the Punch and Judy, then,"

agreed Robin, "and I shall be willing. For never have I seen anything so funny."

"For that only, then," said the friar, and went to find John who had been playing tunes and earning a few extra farthings from the dancers.

By night of that day they reached an abbey set in a hollow. Its square tower stood above the trees in sign of welcome to the travelers, who were most grateful for the hospitality of the abbot. He told them of the best road to their destination and of the deep wood through which they would pass.

There was frost on the ground when they started out next day. They had been a week on their journey and according to the abbot's counsel they had still two days or more to go. Great rolling hills began to appear, and over them hung clouds filled with rain.

And rain it did before the hour was out. Then, when they had begun to enter the wood that embraced the hill, it slackened and the sun came out.

"Let us halt here for our midday food," said John, whose jerkin was wet because his cloak had been left hanging out the window of the White Hart. "Here I shall build a fire to warm us and dry our clothes."

"Let us hope we are not overtaken by marauding Welsh," said the friar hopefully, "for we are at the border. We shall say the office, to remind us in Whose care we are, here as well as everywhere."

They knelt in the woods, as if it had been a cathedral, as indeed it looked to be. For the trees, bare of leaves, arched overhead in the very same way that the groined arches of stone swept up high overhead in the Gothic churches. "Maybe that is where the idea came from," thought Robin.

The fire felt comforting and warm. There was no ale and only one withered apple left, but water flowed in the river hard by, from which John filled the leather flagons. After they had eaten, John sang a ballad while he dried his clothes. When Robin asked if he might try the harp, John showed him how to hold it and pluck the strings, but it was not so easy as it appeared. John promised to teach him.

"By all accounts," said Brother Luke, "this forest goeth for miles, and it may well be that we shall not come out of it by nightfall."

"Now I remember this wood," said John, nodding his head, "though it was but once I went through it. It is of great size, but there is a woodman's cottage I recall wherein we can shelter for the night. I found the woodman and his goodwife courteous and kindly folk, willing to share what they have."

"Let us be on our way," said Robin, "now that we are

near to our journey's end. I wish to see my godfather Sir Peter de Lindsay. Think you he is a good man as my father says, John-go-in-the-Wynd? Will he want me now to stay with him? For how shall I be an esquire or even a page?" Robin was thoughtful.

"It is well known in the country roundabout that he is a gracious master and a noble knight," said John. "His lady, too, is well loved for her goodness to the poor."

"Fear not, my son," the friar assured him. "Thou'lt find kind friends in thy new home."

All afternoon the way continued through the forest, yet there was no sign of its coming to an end. The dusk began to fall, and the howl of a wolf sent shivers down Robin's spine. Still no woodman's hut appeared and there was nought but forest trees and brush on every hand.

Finally, when it was so dark they could hardly see the path, Robin pointed out a feeble light. "See, there, through the trees," he said, "a small cottage. That must be the place."

"Ah," John sighed in relief, "then I was not mistaken. It is the woodman's cottage where we shall lodge tonight."

"How welcome the hearth and fire will be," declared Brother Luke. "Let us hope we shall be as welcome."

"By my faith, if we be not welcome, then the serf is an ingrate. For when I passed this way before, I helped yon woodman bind up the wound he'd got from a fallen ax. Then I carried him on my back to the cot, where the woman tended him."

The woodcutter and his wife made them welcome and shared gladly what they had. The ale was well brewed and there was pease porridge and bread for supper. Then John played the little harp and sang.

The next morning, well refreshed, the three voyagers set out on the last leg of their journey. The weather was neither fair nor rainy, neither hot nor cold, but somewhere in between, "as English weather is like to be," said the friar.

When true daylight arrived, they had come to the edge of the wood, and now the hills stood all about, being very high toward the north, where the Welsh mountains loomed in the blue distance.

For the most part the road lay low among the hills, winding in and out, following the river. A heavy mist hung over the valley so thick it was like a white blanket which parted only enough for the next step to be seen, then closed in again. When wayfarers were met, it was as if they had appeared by magic, out of nowhere. Once, where the road was narrow, a group of peasants suddenly came out of the mist and stopped to ask their way. Their speech was very strange to Robin, but John-go-in-the-Wynd seemed to know what they said, for he directed them in the same strange tongue.

"They are Welsh," he explained, "and have wandered out of their way in the fog. My mother was Welsh, so I know some of the words. There is much trouble with the Welsh along the border here, but these seemed like harmless folk."

Late in the afternoon a breeze suddenly sprang up. In a few moments the mists lifted and the air cleared. Robin looked up in amazement, for there, rising high against the racing clouds, stood a town with a church tower and castle complete. It must be, it was, Lindsay!

"Look!" he cried. "Look! There it is! We have arrived."

" 'Tis true," agreed John. " 'Tis as I hoped. We have arrived before sundown and can enter the castle before the gate is closed."

"Now thanks be to Him who guided us aright," said Brother Luke devoutly, blessing himself.

"Lindsay it is, surely," said John, "for only Lindsay stands so, on a mound ringed with hills, like a pudding in a saucer. We've but to cross yon bridge, go up the hill and through the town gate, and we are there. From the market cross 'tis but a step to the castle gate. It is a happy end to our journey. Beyond the town and castle lives my own mother."

They crossed the bridge and started up the hill. Now that he was so near to his destination, Robin dreaded the meeting with Sir Peter. What sort of welcome would he have, limping as he was on crutches? What sort of page could he be, having no free hands for service?

Robin need not have been afraid. As soon as they had passed through the outer gate, a messenger went swiftly ahead of the travelers to announce them. The drawbridge was down and the gate opened to them without question, and they were received in the Great Hall as if they had been emissaries of the King.

Sir Peter was scarcely recovered from his wounds. He sat in a high-backed chair near the fire, while Lady Constance sat at her embroidery frame with a small girl leaning against her knee. Nearby were her ladies and two little boys who romped with the hounds.

When the travelers entered the Hall, Lady Constance rose, and, drawing the children about her, stood beside Sir Peter to greet them.

"It is a true pleasure to welcome you into our household," said Sir Peter to Robin, not seeming to notice that Robin could not straighten. "We are grateful to this good friar for his care of you, and to John-go-in-the-Wynd who is known to us. This is Lady Constance and our daughter Alison, and these are my two sons, Henry and Richard."

Lady Constance warmly embraced Robin, crutches and

all. "We have long awaited your coming, dear child, and now we are most happy that you have safely arrived."

"I shall make a sorry page, my lady," said Robin ruefully. "But I can sing and I can read a little to while away the time for your lordship," he offered, "and I can pen letters for you."

Sir Peter kept Robin's hand in his and spoke directly to him. "Each of us has his place in the world," he said. "If we cannot serve in one way, there is always another. If we do what we are able, a door always opens to something else."

There it was again, Robin thought, a door. He wondered whether Sir Peter meant the same thing that Brother Luke had intended.

Each of the travelers was assigned to his own place. Robin was to have a chamber in the keep. The friar was to be lodged in a little room over the chapel in the inner ward of the castle, and John-go-in-the-Wynd was given quarters over the outer entrance gate. Before leaving the Hall he asked a favor.

"By your leave," he said, "I would like to visit my old mother, who lives not far away. But I shall stay here awhile until my young master finds his way about."

Now that he was well received, Robin found everything about Lindsay exciting and interesting. The view from the top of the keep where they went in the morning was breathtaking.

"I can see for miles in every direction," he said excitedly. "Surely no enemy could attack without being seen by the Watch."

"Didst forget the fog?" asked John-go-in-the-Wynd, who had accompanied him.

"And look yonder," said Adam the bowman, who stood

watch that day. "See that tiny moving spot in the field?"

At first Robin could not find anything that moved in the open field to which Adam pointed. Then he was just able to make out the figure of a shepherd and a flock of sheep. After a great deal of Adam's directing and pointing he could see a woodcutter emerging from the trees by the river.

"By night, or under cover of mist," said Adam, "a whole army could creep over hill and through forest without being seen. 'Tis from the north and west that we look for trouble. Lord Jocelyn to the west hath long coveted this domain. And Sir Hugh Fitzhugh, to the north yonder, who is cousin to Sir Peter, hath a quarrel with him."

"But they could not take so strong a castle, surely," said Robin.

"We can be starved out," said Adam.

From the other side of the tower Robin could look down upon the town and the church roof, and see clearly how the church was shaped like a cross. He could see the roof of the market cross in the open square, and the people walking about. He could see the bend of the river and the two bridges, one leading west and the one to the south, where they had crossed yesterday. To the north the ground fell straight away down to the river more than a hundred feet below.

"My mother's cottage is there," said John, pointing north. "Over the hill and into the next valley."

Robin could see where the tower of the village church showed above the trees. Beyond, he could see the manor house against a dark forest which crowned the hills far, far away.

"Is it near to the village, where yon church tower stands?" asked Robin.

"Aye, 'tis just there this side of the church. A tidy bit of a house on the heath where she lives alone with her cat. There is a path all the way. If thou'rt to call upon her she would bake thee a bannock."

Robin repeated the directions, but laughed at the thought of going all that way to make a visit.

"Go you by that road I see leading up from the river here?" he asked again.

"No," said John, "for 'tis a long way round by Letham Bridge. I go through the town and by the drovers' road and across the ford beyond."

It was more difficult for Robin to go down the circular stair from the top of the keep than it had been to go up. Each step was set on a center newel, and the steps fanned out from it. Robin had to keep to the outside wall to allow room for the crutches to spread far enough to bear his weight. John went ahead of him to catch him in case he should fall.

"I shall get the way of it soon," said Robin. Before the day was out, he found it easier. They had gone up and down stair after stair; up to the watchtowers and the belfry of the chapel. To the kitchens and storerooms, to the armory and down to the dungeons.

Then John took Robin to the stables to see the horses. There were dappled Percherons from France and shire geldings of tremendous size built to bear the weight of men in armor. There were lighter animals for hunting, hawking, and riding, and others still smaller, like the jennet Robin had ridden. Robin thought the gray one looked like his father's favorite.

How he wished he might ride it, going astride properly, as he should. Would he ever again be able to mount a horse? Would he be able to practice in the tilting yard, or go ahawking? Would he ever stand straight and tall?

Last of all, they went to the workshop near the stables. There the yew bows were made and repaired; staves for lances and pikestaffs were cut. Such small things as plates, cups, bowls, and platters were made by the turners in the town. Arrows were made by the fletchers.

"It is here we shall make the little harp," said John.

"Can we make it soon?" asked Robin.

"We shall begin tomorrow if I can find the wood," promised John.

As soon as Robin was settled in the household of the castle, he was taken in hand again by Brother Luke, who laid out a plan of study and recreation for him that would fit in with the duties assigned him as page. Sir Peter had explained that he would expect Robin to attend to everything which it was possible for him to do. Part of each day was spent with Adam the yeoman shooting at a mark. Part of the day in studying Latin. Evenings after supper the household servants, pages, craftsmen, and all those not on watch gathered about the fire in the Great Hall where Piers Nitingale or John told tales or sang ballads. Each day the friar took Robin down the long path to the river to swim. The water was cold as ice and swift flowing, but now Robin had learned to grit his teeth and plunge in.

It should have been one of his duties to serve at the high table where Sir Peter and the Lady Constance sat with other members of the family and visiting nobles. But because it was so difficult for him to carry things, he was excused from that and was required only to see that his lady was well looked after and the little boys were helped with the cutting of their meat and breaking of the bread for "sopping."

One of the hounds that searched for bones among the straw litter learned to come to Robin for tidbits, seeming to know that he had found a special friend. Robin was careful to find bones from the joint with juicy bits of meat still clinging to them, and soon he was Robin's friend. He even slept by Robin's bed instead of near the fire in the Hall with the other dogs, and followed him everywhere. His name was D'Ath, because he had been brought from a town in Flanders of that name.

ONE DAY, late in October, as the friar walked with Robin along the side of the hill leading down to the river, D'Ath following, Robin stopped in the path.

"Think you it is really helping my legs to swim?" he asked anxiously. "I cannot straighten my back, and can walk only as before, halfway bent over. What think you, Brother Luke, shall I ever straighten?"

"I know not what to think about that." Brother Luke sighed. Then he lifted his head and said firmly, "God alone knows whether thou'lt straighten or no. I know not. But this I tell thee. A fine and beautiful life lies before thee, because thou hast a lively mind and a good wit. Thine arms are very strong and sturdy. Swimming hath helped to make them so, but only because thou hast had the will to do it. Fret not, my son. None of us is perfect. It is better to have crooked legs than a crooked spirit. We can only do the best we can with what we have. That, after all, is the measure of success: what we do with what we have. Come, let us go on."

Robin nodded slowly, then said hopefully,

"Peter the bowman says I have a good arm for the bow and a keen eye for the mark. I can put an arrow up quite well for a beginner, he says."

"And how goeth the woodworking?" asked the friar.

"John-go-in-the-Wynd is helping me to shape the base of the little Saxon harp. It is to be almost like his but is to have my own mark. Where the front block holds the thin maple in a curve, his is plain. Mine shall have tracery. He bent the maple around an oval-shaped form whilst it was green. And meantime, John is showing me how to shape and smooth the post which is the upright. It, too, is of maple, but it is well seasoned and beautifully marked. From a deer that Adam the bowman killed we are drying gut for the strings."

"Thou'rt becoming a true craftsman," said the friar. "And wilt be able to play the harp when 'tis done?"

"Already I can pick out part of the tune of 'Ca' the Yaws' and can sing it as well. It is sad, but pleasant to hear. When I learn it all I shall sing it for my Lady Constance. And when I see my mother again, I shall sing it for her." Robin stopped for a moment, then went on thoughtfully,

"Think you my mother will know me when she sees me thus?"

"Thy mother will know and love thee always, my son," the friar assured him. "Whether thou'rt bent or straight, well or ill, knight or clerk, lord or minstrel."

When would he see his mother? Where was she now?

October had passed in lingering summer warmth. But with the coming of November there was often fog and rain. When it cleared, raw winds swept down from the north, whistling through corridors and hall, sending up whirls of dust in the courtyard, billowing the tapestries that hung on the wall.

Brother Luke took Robin each day, as before, to swim. They followed the path to a place near Letham Bridge. "It will be good for thee even in the chilly autumn weather," he comforted, when Robin shivered at the thought of the icy water. "It sends the blood flying through thy veins to warm thee. Besides, it strengthens thy body and, best of all, it strengthens thy spirit to do a hard thing."

Robin was now quite strong, although he could not straighten. He was able to go about easily from keep to tower, from hall to chapel, from turret to dungeon. Even the twisting stairs held no terror for him, because he had learned to place the crutches carefully and swiftly where they would hold and balance him. He could play games with the boys in the courtyard, shooting at a mark, hide-and-go-seek, and duck on a rock. Robin's keen eye and strong arms helped him to send the "duck," a small pointed stone, so far he could easily get to the goal and back before the other boys could retrieve the duck.

"Aw, no fair!" cried Denis one day. "You can go twice as fast as we can on those seven-league boots of yours." Robin only laughed and played the harder.

Many times a day he went in and out the castle gate, and he had already made friends with Alan-at-Gate. Alan was a gruff old fellow, for he was long hours in attendance on duty and was responsible for the safety of all within the castle. He challenged everyone who passed, whether going in or coming out, demanding to know his business. Robin soon learned that Alan-at-Gate had a soft side as well as a rough one. Once, when he had come on Alan unawares, he heard him playing the flageolet. Robin told him about the Saxon harp he was making. Robin discovered, too, that Alan liked sweets, so he kept a good supply of honey cakes in his pocket for largess. He was allowed to come and go through the gate whenever he liked, with D'Ath at his heels.

"Now that the castle is well known to thee, and thou'rt well started on making the harp, it is time for me to visit my old mother," said John-go-in-the-Wynd to Robin. "Dost know how to go on with the harp?"

"Yes, I am sure I do," Robin answered. "It is a secret I wish to keep, and if I need help, Brother Luke can give it me. William Wise the Farrier is making the tool of hardened iron, as you asked him to do. I shall be careful to make the holes and the pegs for the strings to fit. Let me see once more how they go and how many there are."

John showed Robin the graceful instrument and how the seven strings were fastened with tiny pegs in the maple sounding board which covered the hollow oval base. He showed him how they were drawn tightly to the upper arm of the harp by wooden keys which just fitted the tapered holes tightly enough so they stayed whichever way they were turned.

" 'Twill not be easy to get the keys exactly like the holes," he cautioned.

"No," said Robin, "but I can do it. I know I can."

"Thou canst but try," said John. "Anyone can *not* do it."

Robin went with John across the courtyard to the outer gate.

"Dost know where to find me in case of need?" asked John.

"Yes," said Robin, mimicking the way John had told it to him. " ' 'Tis over the path beyond the river, across yon field, and through the forest, then fording the stream and up another field, through another wood, and 'tis just there this side of the church in the village of Tripheath. A tidy bit of a house on the heath where she lives with her cat, and if thou'rt there, she'd bake thee a bannock.' "

John laughed.

"That's the right of it," he agreed. "And now, farewell, young master."

John slung his pack and the harp across his back and was gone.

Early that same day mists began to rise, which later became a thick fog. Little could be seen from watchtower or wall but a blank whiteness covering everything. Even the outer walls of the castle were hidden from the watchman at the top of the keep. When Robin crossed the outer bailey, going from the workshop along the wall to the inner castle gate, he could see only a few steps ahead. Sometimes he could scarcely see D'Ath, who was close at his heels. Sometimes heads appeared out of nowhere, or legs walked along as if they were unattached. When Robin reached the drawbridge and started to cross, Alan-at-Gate's voice shouted the challenge. Even though the voice was familiar, it sounded ghostlike and strange to Robin as it came out of the fog.

"*Who goes there?*" said the voice.

" 'Tis I, Robin," came the answer, as Robin crossed the moat and passed under the portcullis.

"This be a treacherous cloud of mist," said Alan-at-Gate, as Robin entered.

"Will there be danger in it, think you?" asked Robin.

"Aye, danger enough," said Alan gravely. "The Welsh, yonder, long have wanted this castle, for it be strong. Now, with fog to help, and so few to guard the walls, there is chance they might get it, God forbid."

"If my father would only come with his men, it would be safe," declared Robin. "He is the strongest knight in the King's bodyguard, and Elfred the Dane is his finest bowman. Elfred can shoot out the eyes of an owl at two hundred paces." While he boasted Robin's eyes shone. "But," he ended sadly, "neither Elfred nor my father is here."

When supper was served in the Great Hall that evening there were few gathered to eat it, because every man was on guard, and only the womenfolk and the children kept Sir Peter company. The two pages, Denis and Lionel, attended them, and Robin, as usual, sat between Lady Constance and the two little boys.

D'Ath and the other hounds seemed ill at ease. They paced up and down the hall, settled themselves in the rushes on the floor, only to rise and begin walking about again.

"Down, D'Ath!" commanded Robin.

"Quiet, Roy! Be still, Nance!" Denis ordered.

They dropped to the floor for a moment, but were soon moving about again. Not even the bones kept them quiet for more than a short time.

Lady Constance talked pleasantly with her ladies, but

Sir Peter seemed to be always listening. While they were still at table there was a sudden commotion. Shouts and cries from the inner ward came up through the windows and a sound of running feet pounding along the passage. Sir Peter started from his chair.

Adam the Yeoman came bursting into the Hall, so hurried with ill news that he scarcely stopped to bob his head before speaking.

"Your Lordship," he began, out of breath, "we are attacked. The Welsh are hammering at the town gate. They have slain the watch by creeping close to the wall in the fog. They waited for him to turn, then put an arrow in his back."

" 'Tis come, then," said Sir Peter, reaching for the great sword which hung on the wall. "What strength are they? Is it known?"

"It is hard to say," said Adam. "They make a great noise about the walls, but nought can be seen for the fog. They have built fires under the south gate and flambeaux glow on all sides, so I fear we are surrounded."

"Gather every man not armed into the inner bailey, where they will be provided with longbows and arrows," directed Sir Peter. To Lady Constance he said, "You, my dear wife, gather all the women and children into the keep. Have them bring clothing and pallets. There, at least, we have water in the well and 'tis a strong fortress."

"Yes, my husband," Lady Constance said obediently, rising and gathering the children to her, while her ladies hastily collected embroidery frames, cloaks, and fripperies. The two pages, Denis and Lionel, carried the food from the table, then took the table boards from the trestles and transferred everything to the hall of the keep. The keep was close to the gatehouse between the inner and outer ward, so there was great excitement in the courtyard.

"What can I do?" asked Robin.

"Will you care for the little boys?" asked Lady Constance. "Little Alison shall come with us."

"Yes," promised Robin. "Each can hold to my jerkin, so we shall keep together among the yeomen."

When the boys had been safely delivered to the keep, Robin remembered the little harp which lay unfinished in the workshop under the south wall. He must get it and keep it safe, too.

Before morning the walls of the town had been breached, and before the day was out the town was taken. When the portcullis of the outer bailey of the castle was raised to admit the yeomen, the townspeople swarmed in. Alan-at-Gate directed the dropping of the heavy iron gate, and it came down so quickly that the last man to enter narrowly missed having his head chopped off.

THE FOG held for days. The Welsh could not get beyond the outer wall of the castle, and the English inside could not tell what strength the enemy possessed. They might be encamped on the surrounding hills, or they might be only a small company. Several of the guards on the wall had been injured, and sometimes the yeomen could tell that an arrow had struck home in the enemy's camp. Most of the time there was only watchful waiting on both sides. The Welsh had a machine for catapulting stones, most of which thudded harmlessly into the courtyard. Sometimes one struck the inner wall, but most of them fell short, dropping into the moat.

Inside the keep women occupied themselves with spinning, weaving, and embroidery. It helped the time to pass more quickly. The children played with toy soldiers and blocks, with hobbyhorses and with dolls. Sometimes Robin told them tales, or sang songs, but he spent most of the time in the chamber where he slept, working on the Saxon harp.

William Wise had set up a workbench for him and had finished the tool of hardened iron. There was a small lathe for turning the keys and a vise all arranged so that Robin could sit on a stool to reach them. The tool for making the holes was sharp, so that part was not difficult.

Just as John-go-in-the-Wynd had said, it was harder

to turn the keys on the lathe so they would fit exactly. They were either too large and would not go in, or, when they had been turned smaller, they were too small and would not hold the strings in tune.

But Robin was learning patience. He had found out that the harder it was to do something, the more comfortable he felt after he had done it.

Sir Peter had stood all of one night on the bastion directing and encouraging the men. They had managed to drive off a raiding party that was trying to scale the wall. Now he was in bed with a chill, and Lady Constance waited upon him.

The food in the larder dwindled, and there were many people to be fed. Besides the garrison and the household there were the yeomen from the town and those who had sought refuge when the portcullis was raised.

Usually there was a good supply of salt fish kept in barrels, but fish had not been plentiful the past summer, so now the supply was meager. There was mutton, to be sure, but it was all on four legs and scattered over the downs beyond the castle and town. The winter kill had not taken place because they waited for freezing weather. There was flour to last for a short time, but the yearly portion from the peasants' holdings was to have been brought to the castle the following week. Besides, there had been a small crop of grain because of the summer's drought.

Then the water began to fail. As Robin came into the Hall at suppertime he passed the table where the retainers sat. Denis leaned to whisper in the ear of Adam the Yeoman.

"There is scarce a foot of water in the well," he whispered. "Just now as I drew it to fill this ewer the cook told me."

"How came this?" asked Adam. " 'Tis known that this

is a good well. Tell not her ladyship, and send the word around that the water must be used sparingly, or 'twill not last the week out, even for drinking." He thought a moment, then said,

"Someone must go for help, or we shall be forced to surrender the castle. It might be that Sir Hugh Fitzhugh would come to our aid, for he, too, is in danger from the Welsh if they break our defense. But whom shall we spare? All are needed at their posts."

"Let me go," said Robin. "I can go out the small door at the north whilst it is early morning. No one will suspect me. They think me a poor shepherd. I shall borrow a smock from William the Farrier's son, and if I am seen, I shall appear stupid. We shall keep it secret, for if Sir Peter were to find out my plan he would forbid me to go, not knowing how strong I am."

"But thou'rt only a lad!" Adam objected, "and art cumbered with crutches as well. And how wilt thou cross the river? The bridge is well guarded at both ends."

"I shall go well, never fear," Robin assured them confidently. "I have it all in my head how it shall be done. I shall find John-go-in-the-Wynd at his mother's cottage in Tripheath village. John shall set forth from there for Sir Hugh and his men. Now, let us plan. First, I want you, Denis, to bring me the smock, and some rags to wrap about my legs. Then, see you, find me a hood that is worn and faded. Besides, I shall need long leather thongs to tie the crutches to my back, for I shall swim the river."

"Fear you not the soldiery?" queried Denis anxiously. "Will you not fall down the steep bank? 'Tis a far distance to the bottom of the ravine, and——" He stopped suddenly, because one of the maids appeared.

"See to it," said Robin with a quick nod.

That evening there was no gathering about the fire. Everyone was restless. The hounds were still uneasy, walking about, cocking their ears at the least sound.

Lady Constance took one of her women to examine the stores. Robin was afraid she would discover how low the water was in the well. Instead, she seemed confident that there was sufficient.

"How fortunate we are that there is plenty of water," she said. "Sir Peter says that our well has never failed."

Denis looked at Robin, knowing that he shared the secret.

Denis, knowing Robin's plan, was in a fidget to be through with his duties and find William the Farrier's son and borrow his clothes. He would probably be with his father at the forge, repairing pikes and lances and heating oil for pouring onto the enemy in case they should pierce the outer castle wall.

Robin put on his warmest under tunic and carefully put away the little harp and all the parts and tools so that they would be safe. He looked at it regretfully, hating to leave it.

Then, when all was ready except changing his clothes, he sought out Brother Luke, for he knew that the friar would give him help and encouragement.

Dressed in the patched and ragged smock, his legs wound about with bits of rag to hold the ill-fitting hosen, Robin tried to sleep away the early part of the night, but excitement kept him wakeful. Even when he dozed, he was aware of what he was about to do. He counted over all the things he must remember. He must go softly with the crutches. He must remember the leather thongs. As Brother Luke had told him, he mustn't forget oil for the rusty lock of the door in the wall. He must keep D'Ath quiet.

Just before dawn Brother Luke touched him.

"Come, my son," he whispered. "We shall say the office before it is time to set forth on thy mission."

When the prayers were finished, Robin pulled on the faded hood, tucked the leather thong inside it, and followed the friar. D'Ath rose from sleep to follow after, but Robin touched his head and whispered a command for him to stop.

"D'Ath, stay you here," he said, wishing very much that the dog could go with him.

They went down a half flight of steps and across the hall of the keep to the winding stair, making their way quietly among the sleeping servants. They went very slowly, for Robin's crutches tapped an alarm when he made haste, and the least misstep would have sent him clattering down.

There was still fog when they came into the open, but it had begun to drift and there was a gray dawn just beginning to break.

"Who goes there?" demanded the sentry at the door, but seeing Robin and the friar, he allowed them to pass, thinking they were bent on some holy errand.

Robin shuddered.

"Art fearful, my son?" asked the friar.

"Not truly," answered Robin, "though 'tis weird in the fog."

"Aye, 'tis an eerie feeling to be out in the cheerless dawn, not knowing at what moment an enemy may appear out of the fog," agreed Brother Luke. And at that moment a face did appear, but it was only one of the guards, who thought the two were on their way to the chapel.

They reached the sally port in the north wall without meeting anyone else. Brother Luke dripped oil into the lock before trying to open the door.

Robin listened.

"Hark!" he whispered. "I hear the Welsh sentry outside. We can count the paces and can tell how far away he is. One, two, three, four——" They counted forty paces. "Now!"

Slowly the door opened and Robin slipped outside.

"Benedicite," whispered the friar in blessing, and closed the door.

Quickly Robin moved away from the door and the wall. In a moment he was at the edge of the deep ravine. He could hear the river far below but could not see it for the fog.

Now began the dangerous descent. Carefully Robin tested each clod of earth, each bit of stone, before trusting his weight to the crutches, praying the while that the fog would hold. Sometimes he slid on his haunches, sometimes seedling trees held him till he was able to find sure footing.

"If I should start a stone rolling," he thought, "the whole Welsh army will be upon my neck."

It seemed hours to Robin that he was sliding, groping, laboring down the treacherous cliff, but it was only a few moments, for the light of morning had scarcely changed when he reached the bottom and found himself at the edge of the river.

He stopped only long enough to fasten the crutches onto his back with the leathern thong and to wind his hood into a kind of hat that perched on top of his head. Then he plunged into the icy water, not allowing himself to consider whether he had the courage to do it.

When first the water closed over him Robin thought he could not bear it. The crutches were awkward. His chest felt tightly squeezed, and as if sharp knives pierced him. He seemed unable to breathe, and his head felt ready to burst. But he struck out fiercely, and after a few strokes began to breathe more easily. Warmth crept through his body and a feeling of power, as if nothing could be too difficult for him. He swam strongly across the swift current toward the path he had seen from the top of the tower.

What if the enemy should be camped on the other side? Suppose they wouldn't believe he was the poor shepherd he pretended to be? Suppose he found it impossible to get up the bank on the other side?

"Anyone could *not* do it," he said to himself stubbornly, and thrashed his arms more fiercely.

At last he felt the stones of shallower water under his feet, the bank appeared mistily green, and he was able to hold himself steady with one hand while he untied the crutches and set them under his armpits. The bank was not very steep after all, and in a moment he was at the top, ready to go on. His teeth chattered in the rising wind.

His feet felt as if they had been frozen. His hands were so numb with cold he could hardly hold the crutches to steady them as he walked. He paused long enough to let down the hood into its proper shape. The warm wool felt good, although it was wet along the edges. Then he looked about for signs of the path. It had shown so clearly from the top of the tower. He moved along the bank a few paces where generations of peasants had worn a "highway," and soon came to the path. The fog was lifting somewhat with the wind, and Robin, looking back once, caught sight of the castle he had left behind. He even caught a glimpse of the sentry along the narrow ridge just where he had so lately escaped by the door in the wall.

After passing through a patch of brush and willows Robin came out into a field. He still could not see very far ahead, but the path was straight before him, so he began to swing along as fast as he could, his crutches making great sweeping circles, his feet covering the ground in tremendous strides. There seemed to be no one about, so he made haste without regard to noise, and gradually the numbness in his hands and feet began to ease. Across the field he went, swing-step, swing-step, swing-step.

The fog wavered and lifted, swirled about in sudden drafts, floated across the path in thin layers, showed a patch of blue sky for an instant and glimpses of trees ahead.

Suddenly a voice rang out.

"*Who goes there?*"

Robin stopped.

" 'Tis but I, Robin," he answered in a meek voice, and the chill that ran down his spine was not all from the dampness of his clothing.

"Robin who?" the voice went on.

"Robin—Crookshank, some call me," answered Robin.

The fog parted, showing the fierce and scowling head of a man.

The guard drew near where he could see the boy.

"Aah," he said. "Art tha' but a shepherd boy, then?" he asked, seeing Robin's poor clothes. "And hast fallen into the river? Come, then, lad, and warm tha'self by the fire. Be not frighted. We'll not hurt thee." He took Robin's arm and tried to draw him toward the camp, which now Robin could see just at the side of the field, for now the fog was fast disappearing. But Robin held back and shook his head, trying to think what he must say and how he must speak.

"Nay," he began, trying to appear stupid, " 'tis na far to the cottage." He edged away, bobbing his thanks, and went on as fast as he dared up the other side of the field and through the hedgerow. He did not stop until he was well beyond earshot of the men in the camp, then stood only for a moment to draw long, steadying breaths.

He chuckled at the way he had fooled the Welshman.

From that point on the path led through a wood and downward toward the valley of a stream which joined the one surrounding the castle. There were no cottages near at hand, but across the stream and beyond a low-lying field and a rising slope Robin could see the wood that extended to the edge of the village where the church tower stood. The sky now was filled with fast-flying clouds and the fog was gone. The stream was shallow enough for Robin to go across on foot and the little wetting he got was nothing after swimming the river.

The wood behind him hid Robin from the camp in the field, for which he was thankful, because the rising ground slowed his going, and he felt as if he were a fair target for arrows. It seemed as if he would never come to the top of the field and the hedgerow separating it from the forest beyond. When he reached the shelter of the great trees, Robin sank down into a bed of bracken to rest. He was very tired.

When breathing was easier and the pain of effort but a dull ache, Robin rose to go on. How much farther had he to go? Would John be there when he arrived? Would he be able to get help in time?

Even through the forest the path was well marked, because it was one that had been used for centuries. The peasants went over it to and from the villages to gather wood or to pasture the sheep.

In about an hour the forest began to thin, and Robin could see the blue smoke coming from the cotters' chimney pots. Which cottage belonged to John's mother? Robin remembered that John had said it was on the heath and near the church. He could see such a cottage from where he stood, so he made his way toward it hopefully. It was so exciting to be within sight of help that Robin forgot that he was tired and hungry, he forgot that he was still cold from his dousing in the river and the fright he'd had. He began to cut across the heath toward the cottage but had not gone far when John himself came out of the door.

Robin stopped.

"John!" he called at the top of his voice. "*John! Oh, John*-go-in-the-Wy-y-y-nd."

John heard him and looked his way, then came running.

"Master Robin!" he exclaimed. "What's amiss? How came thou here?"

Without waiting for an answer he grasped Robin's crutches and swept him up into his arms, because he could see that Robin had come as far as he was able. It had been Robin's plan to issue orders as his father might have done; to have been lordly and commanding. But it was such a relief to be cared for and to have the weight of his body taken from his aching armpits that he allowed John to carry him, and said not a word until he was laid upon the straw pallet.

An old woman stood by the fire stirring something in a pot. She looked at Robin but didn't speak. A cat mewed and coaxed her, rubbing against her skirts.

"The castle is in danger!" said Robin at once. "The Welsh have taken the town and are at the gates of the outer bailey. The food is giving out. The water low in the well. You must get help. You must get it soon."

"But how came thou here?" said John, amazed. "How didst escape the sentry?" John was already putting on his hood and fastening his leather jerkin.

He went on without waiting.

"Knowest what force the Welsh have?"

"No," said Robin, "the fog has kept us from seeing. But whenever we tried to make a sally into the town, we were forced back."

"I shall be gone straight away. Stay thou here for safety and to rest."

John-go-in-the-Wynd was well named, for go he did, closing the door behind him almost before he had finished speaking.

Robin sighed. It was good to be able to rest.

"Come, now," said the woman, as she took off Robin's clothes to dry them. "Thou'lt be famished with hunger. I'll bake thee a bannock." As tired as he was, Robin grinned. She went to the cupboard and took out a flat cake which she put on a hot stone to bake.

Robin slept after the woman fed him and didn't wake until the sun was low in the west. The sound of the door opening was what really woke him. It was John.

Robin was up on his elbow in a second.

"Did you not go then?" he asked in bewilderment. Then he realized he had slept and that it was late in the day. "Did you find help then?"

"Yes, already they are well on their way from my lord Hugh Fitzhugh's castle," said John. "A large force of foot soldiers and a company of lancers go by the drovers' road, one company by the way through wood and field and another going around to attack from the other side of the town by way of Letham Bridge. It hath been agreed that we shall give the signal from the bell tower of the church. There are no better bowmen in England. The siege will be lifted. Thou'lt see!"

"I want to see it," declared Robin. "I want to see it all!"

"See it thou shalt," promised John. "Now, Mither, serve forth yon porridge, for I have not broken my fast this day."

The mother bustled about, putting the porridge into a bowl for all to dip into and drawing a bench up to the table.

John laid out the little harp, put bread into his pouch, and stuck a knife in his belt. "I am no warrior," he said to Robin. "I am but a messenger and minstrel. But who knows? I might find myself close to the enemy. Closer than I would like," he added with a shrug.

The meal was soon over, and they made ready to start.

"Think you I can go so far again this day?" asked Robin anxiously.

"Thou hast no need to think of that," John assured him. "I can carry thee right well, as the good friar did. The harp and the crutches we shall strap on so they will not cumber us." He fastened the crutches to his side and the harp around Robin's neck, so it hung down his back. "Soon thou'lt be carrying thine own harp, God willing."

"Fare thee well, old Mother," said John, embracing her. "Up, now, young master," he said to Robin, and with that they left the cottage and went on their way.

"How shall we go?" asked Robin, as John strode down

the path on the way out of the village. "Shall we go by the way I came here? Or by way of Letham Bridge?"

"Neither," answered John-go-in-the-Wynd. "I know still another way. I know a path leading through the forest to the southeast. It goeth past the priory where we shall ford the river. We can come at the town easily from there. Then we can wait for nightfall, and indeed it will be nightfall ere we arrive, but there will be a moon.

"We shall creep along the river, under cover of the reeds and willows, and enter the town through the shoemaker's house, which is on the wall. He is known to me, and we have a signal between us. He knoweth the sound of my harp, and the certain tune I play will tell him we have need of him. From there it is quite simple to get into the graveyard of the church, thence into the church itself, and into the tower. There we shall see all and hear all if we are not deafened by the bells."

"What an adventure to tell my father!" cried Robin.

Although he carried Robin, John trotted along at a good speed, for he knew every curve in the path. It was only a short way to the ford of the river, near the priory, and from there across fields covered with grazing sheep to the forest. There they rested. When they reached the top of the hill beyond, John pointed out the drovers' road far below. There, glints of light on lance and pennant, helmet, and moving figures showed Robin the fast-moving company of soldiers. Because it was nearly dusk and suppertime, blue smoke rose from every chimney pot in the village they had left, and in the low places mist began to rise.

"We must make haste," said John, lifting Robin again to his back, "or we shall be too late."

When they had to cross open country again, John kept to the hedgerows so they would not be seen, and as they came nearer to Lindsay, he kept well away from every barn and outbuilding.

"For aught we know the Welsh may be encamped out here on this side of the castle as well as on the other," he explained. "They might question even a minstrel such as I. 'Tis safer for our skins to go softly."

By the time they reached the place where the drovers' road led, John halted before crossing the road to observe the sentry. They waited for the sound of his footsteps to die away around the town. The moon was high, and by keeping well in the shadow of a tree they were able to cross the road without being seen.

"Ah," said John with a sigh of relief. "So far we have come safely. Soon Sir Hugh's men will encircle the town. By then we shall be in the church tower to give the signal for attack."

"We have not seen the enemy on this side of the town," whispered Robin hopefully.

"No," agreed John. "Because they have taken the town, and will be inside the walls. There is more need of outposts to the south and west, where the two bridges are, and where the roads leading from them are well traveled. The Welsh will reason that there is little likelihood of danger from this road because it is well known that Sir Peter and his cousin Sir Hugh are not on friendly terms. Sir Peter is for the King and for England. Sir Hugh is not. But they are of one family, and were once like brothers. I had little difficulty in persuading him. Sir Hugh."

"Perhaps they will be friends from now on," said Robin. "Perhaps Sir Hugh will be won for the King."

"It may be." John nodded. "Most of the lords in this part of the country are for keeping their lands to themselves. But times are changing, and we have a good king."

"Hark!" whispered Robin again. "All is still. The sentry is at the far end of his walk. Shall we go then?"

"Aye, 'tis time," said John. "Hast the little harp safe?"

" 'Tis safe," said Robin, grasping John about the neck and getting himself settled on his back.

They crept forward again, shielded by the darkness, and made their way along a narrow path that followed the wall until the rising ground told John they were near to the shoemaker's cottage. There again they halted, to make sure no sentry was about. John, letting Robin slip to the ground, fitted the crutches under his arms and took the harp from about his neck.

The tune he played was mournful and slow, but it must have reached the ears of the shoemaker. John was just beginning to play it for the third time when there was an answer to it in the form of a bagpipe jig. Robin could see John bobbing his head up and down happily because his playing had brought forth the right response. There followed another period of waiting while the sentry passed again on the wall. They scarcely breathed until he had turned again and was going the other way. By counting his steps they knew when he was far enough away for them to act.

Then, without warning, a sort of chair was let down from a window high in the wall. John fastened Robin into it and gave the rope a jerk. Robin was hauled aloft so quickly that he had no time to think what he should do or what he should say. He found himself being lifted inside the upper room of a small house and the window drawn to. He faced a little man, who cautioned him to silence while again they waited for the sentry to come and to go.

There was no light in the room except the moonlight that came in through the window.

"This is really exciting," thought Robin.

He wished that John had been able to come into the house with him.

He heard the "tramp, tramp" of the sentry and the thudding of the pikestaff as it struck the stone when the sentry turned at the wall of the house. The sound lessened, and once more the rope was lowered.

This time it was for John. Robin could see the iron wheel under the window which turned like a windlass to let out the rope.

In a moment John stood in the room with him. The rope and iron wheel were stored in an innocent-looking chest. The shoemaker quickly lifted the wheel out of the strong wooden block which held it covered with a flat board and cloth. The shoemaker motioned for Robin and John to follow him down the steep stair leading to the house below.

THEY did not linger in the house, but with a few words to the shoemaker, left by way of the garden. There was a door in the wall leading into the graveyard of the church, where John and Robin slipped quietly from one great tombstone to another. They entered the church by the sanctuary door, startling the sacristan who slept and ate in a small room off the entrance porch.

"Who art thou?" he called, hearing the creak of the door. "Art friend or foe?"

"Hist!" warned John, stepping quickly toward the light of the lantern held by the sacristan. "We are friends. I am John-go-in-the-Wynd, minstrel. This lad is young Master Robin, friend and ward of Sir Peter. He hath this day saved us all." The sacristan held the lantern up where he could see John's face.

"Now I mind thee," he said, nodding his head. "I knew thy father."

John told the sacristan how Robin had come to warn him and to get help, and described the plan he had made with Sir Hugh to sound the bells giving the signal for attack.

"Come with me, then," said the sacristan, leading the way.

They went down the long, dark aisle of the church to the door of the tower.

"Give me thy crutches here, young master," said John. "Canst thou climb the ladder or wilt go pickaback? 'Tis a great height, but there are resting places."

"I can do it," said Robin shortly. Had he not climbed to the towers and turrets of the castle many times?

They had just reached the belfry when it was time for curfew to ring. The bells began an ear-splitting clamor.

"Down flat, and cover thy ears—quick!" shouted John.

They flattened themselves on the platform and endured the deafening sound.

"We shall go to the top first," said John, "for it is yet too soon to give the signal, and from there we shall see somewhat."

From the belfry to the top of the tower it was another thirty feet of climbing. When they reached the top Robin fell in a heap onto the platform with every bit of strength gone from his legs and arms. It slowly returned. In a little while he was able to rise and stand beside John, looking out over the town.

"We agreed that I should wait an hour after curfew, when the moon will be nearly overhead," said John. "That allows time for all companies to be in place, and with the sounding of the bell to move in about the town and castle wall at once."

"How can you tell when it has been an hour?" asked Robin.

"By the feel of it," said John. "Besides, I shall play 'Love a Garland Is' and 'Lament of a Lass.' That will be half of the hour." He unslung the harp from Robin's back and began the music.

While they waited for the rest of the hour to pass, John pointed out the familiar turrets of the castle, the north tower where they had stood that day, and the tower of the keep where the household waited for deliverance. He strummed on the harp between times.

They tried to see into the hills about the town, but saw only the quiet countryside bathed in moonlight. In the town, supper fires sent up blue smoke, and here and there was the red glare of torchlight and campfire. Glints of moonlight on helmet or shield shone from the walls where sentries walked, but very little sound could be heard at that height.

The hour was up.

"Now," said John, "it is time for the alarm. Stay thou here, and I shall return. Cover thy ears well, but watch to see what happens." He was gone through the hatch into the darkness below. Robin waited, his skin prickling with excitement. Would the signal be at the right time? Would the arrows find their mark and lift the siege?

Bong! BONGGG! BONGGG! BONGGG! BONG! BONGGG!!!!

The great bell rang, sending waves of sound that went out over the hills and came echoing back into the stone of the bell tower, which trembled with the vibration.

At first Robin could see nothing different from what he had seen before. Then, it was as if a part of the landscape itself moved off there toward the south, just below the edge of the town. Gathering from the slopes were tiny moving figures, now in the open, now lost in shadow. Robin searched for another sign, this time in the direction of Letham Bridge. The sign was there where he could see more clearly.

John came up, breathing hard.

"What's to be seen?" he asked. "Are they moving? Hast seen any arrows fly?" He looked to the Letham Bridge.

Then it came.

A hail of arrows that were like dark rain sped from oncoming yeomen, dropping the sentries on the bridge and picking off men of the guard manning the wall of the town. From where they stood Robin could see it all as plainly as if it had been a toy village set in a toy landscape, and the soldiers, toy soldiers. He saw pikemen strike down sentries of the enemy at the town gate and take prisoner the Welsh guards. He saw the company of Sir Hugh's men enter and take the town.

It had been a complete surprise.

When John-go-in-the-Wynd saw what was happening and realized that the plan had been successful, he tossed his hat into the air and clasped Robin in his arms

"We've won!" he shouted. "The Welsh are routed! Lindsay is saved once more!"

Then, setting Robin on his feet again, he said,

"Stay thou here, and watch how the Welsh are marched out of the town whilst I go below. Thou'lt hear such a peal of bells as shall nigh wake the dead lying below." Down he went again through the hatch to the belfry.

With the pealing of the bells, flares went up from castle and town, windows and doors opened. The peal of bells stopped. John came back and together they watched the lifting of the siege. They could see people running about through the streets embracing one another, tossing caps and hats into the air, and in other ways showing their joy at being freed of the Welsh invaders. In a short while they saw the enemy marched out of town.

Tears streamed down Robin's cheeks.

"I must not cry," he thought, wiping them away. "Not even for joy."

"Now," said John, lifting Robin aloft, "thou'lt be carried on my shoulder—so. For thou'rt the hero of this victory," and together they went down the long stretches of ladder and stair to the ground.

"Make haste," said Robin. "Let us go to the keep at once, so Sir Peter and Lady Constance shall know that I am safe and well. Brother Luke will be sure of it, for his prayers have followed me this day. That I know."

All the way through the town square John made his way with Robin on his shoulder high above the villagers dancing in the dawn of returning day.

They were greeted with cheers at the castle gate and followed across the courtyard to the inner gate and to the keep by the cheering crowd.

Alan-at-Gate saw them from the gatehouse. The drawbridge was lowered and the portcullis raised, and just inside the whole company of the household stood to receive them. Sir Peter was in the center with his sons and the two pages. Near him was Lady Constance with her women and little Alison. D'Ath whimpered joyfully beside Brother Luke.

Sir Peter held out his arms and helped Robin to the ground, placing the crutches to support him. Then, placing his hand upon Robin's head, he spoke solemnly.

"Now, before God and this company," he said, "I do hail thee Conqueror and true son of thy noble father."

Lady Constance embraced Robin and the women made much of him. D'Ath was too well bred a dog to push himself forward, but his eager prancing and wriggling finally brought him to Robin's side, where he thrust his long, cold nose into Robin's hands.

John-go-in-the-Wynd was called forward. He was given a holding of land for his own and a portion of sheep. With it went certain rights for hunting and fishing to be his and his heirs forever.

Brother Luke gave Robin his blessing and went with him to his chamber.

"It seems long since I left here," said Robin, looking

around as if he expected things to be changed. But there was the cross over his bed, and there on the workbench the little harp just as he had left it, waiting for the strings to be fastened to the keys.

"Much hath happened in this one day," said Brother Luke. "I should like to hear how thy journey went. By thy look, thou hast fared well, except for needing a good wash and a sleep. Off with thy borrowed clothes and once more I shall care for thee."

Sleep overtook Robin even before Brother Luke had finished.

The days grew short and very cold. Everyone went about with a red nose and a cloud of frozen breath. Robin was glad of the woolen gloves made for him by Lady Constance. They were snug and warm and decorated with needlework on the back.

The river ran more slowly now, and ice began to form along the edges. Robin stopped swimming and took his exercise in other ways. He spent a great deal of time with Adam Bowyer shooting at a mark, and was already at work again in the carpentry shop making a viol such as Piers Nitingale used.

The harp was finished. Robin had learned how to tune it by tightening the strings and could play it a little. Brother Luke was teaching him to sing a carol, because it was near to the Feast of Christmas. There would be singing and caroling in the Hall and Robin remembered his father's letter and hoped that Christmas would bring his father and mother to the castle.

One day before the Feast of Thomas the Apostle, and after the Feast of St. Lucy (the thirteenth of December), Robin was with Sir Peter in the armory. The coats of mail, the helmets, the lances, pikes, bows and arrows were being put in order, and the great two-handed sword hung on the wall.

"See you here," said Sir Peter. "This is where the blow struck my helmet. There is a dent as large as a basin." He rubbed his head where the helmet had been thrust in.

Robin ran his fingers around the ugly cavity, imagining how it would feel to be struck with a mace. He was thinking of his father and wondering whether he, too, had been wounded.

"Will the Scottish wars have ended, think you?" he asked.

"I have had no word directly," answered Sir Peter. "There have been rumors about that troops of returning soldiers have been seen. Some were going southward along the highroad. John-go-in-the-Wynd might tell us if he were here, but he has not been nigh the castle for weeks. I dare say he is busy building shelter for his new flocks and gathering wood for the winter that his old mother may be warm."

Robin said no more, but after that he went often to the top of the keep to scan the countryside for signs of horsemen. Sometimes he could see nothing for fog or rain. Sometimes the air was crisp and clear, and he could see far beyond the hills. Once a cloud of dust on the road moving toward the town kept him excited for an hour, but it proved to be only a flock of sheep being driven to market. Once a company of lancers appeared, but they turned southward.

On the afternoon of the Eve of Christmas Robin was at his post on top of the keep, with Adam Bowyer, who was on watch. It began to snow. Robin watched while the silent whiteness covered the hills and the roofs of the town. Far, far below he could see a hawking party. He could see the pages coming from the forest, dragging the yule log and branches of holly to decorate the Hall.

Suddenly Adam Bowyer cried, "Look! Look yonder!" He pointed east, where the road led into the highroad and to the town gate. Robin left the north side of the tower and joined Adam, looking toward where he pointed. The snow dimmed what he saw, but it was clear enough. A company of knights and men at arms rode toward the castle. At the head rode the King, for only he wore the royal colors and the royal quarterings of the banners. At his side rode one who sat his horse as only Robin's father did. In the midst of the great company were ladies, pikemen, men at arms, and yeomen. That must be the Queen. Was it the Lady Maud there beside her in the center? It must be!

Robin burst into a cheer.

"It is true!" he shouted. "It is true! The Scottish wars are over, and my father is alive!" He must say nothing about his mother, for fear Adam would think him babyish. He dashed down the winding stair as fast as he dared, crossed the inner ward to the Hall, thump, slip, thump, slip, and then to the solar to find Sir Peter. Thump, slip, thump, slip, thump, slip, thump, slip!

Sir Peter roared with laughter at Robin's attempt to tell him about the approaching company, for he knew from the moment he had seen Robin's shining face the good news.

"Shall I go to the gate to be there when they enter, think you?" asked Robin anxiously.

"Do what seems best, my boy," said Sir Peter. "Go stand beside Alan-at-Gate or stay you here by my side. I know what a fever of excitement is in thy bones, but do what you most want to do." Robin felt as if he must run to meet the company, must see his father, and feel the comfort of his mother's arms about him. Yet he felt timid about facing either of them. They would find him so changed.

"If I stand beside you, my lord, they will surely know

it is I. If they see me in the courtyard, they may think I am but one of the stableboys. I shall stay here."

"Come, lad," said Sir Peter. "Let us go to the window of the tower. There we can see the company cross the drawbridge, and before they have dismounted we can be back ready to welcome them in the Hall at the head of the stair."

Before leaving the Hall, Sir Peter called Denis the page and sent word to Lady Constance to be ready to greet the noble visitors. He and Robin went quickly up the winding stair to the turret overlooking the drawbridge. They reached it in time to hear the pounding of the hoofs on the timbers of the bridge and to see the waving banners. The handsome erect figure of Sir John de Bureford was fitting

company for the noble-looking King. And there, there—now just passing into the courtyard—was Robin's lovely mother, the veil of her coif floating and mingling with that of the Queen whom she attended.

There was no time for greeting or waving. The tumult of horse and weapon made too much noise for voices to have been heard. Sir Peter grasped Robin and swung him across his back. They went swiftly back the way they had come and were standing in welcome at the head of the great staircase as the company entered.

Who spoke first or what was first said it would be hard to tell. Robin found himself bowing to kiss his mother's hand, then felt her soft arms about him.

"Robin, my Robin," she whispered, and for a moment said no more, but only held him close, as if she could not let him go. The crutches fell to the stone floor with a great clatter. Robin's father bent to pick them up, laughing to keep from showing how deeply he was moved by the sight of them.

"He is my son, too," he said, gently tugging at the mother's close-enfolding arms and holding Robin at arm's length to look into his face.

"You are grown," he said. "Your eyes no longer outrace your chin as do a child's. You've now the look of a youth!" Sir John embraced his son warmly. Nothing was said of crutches or of misshapen legs, or of ill fortune or of good.

Sir Peter spoke. "Shall we not allow our guests to retire?"

"Yes," agreed the King. "Later we shall hear news of the war's ending and how all have fared this long year. Let us go our several ways and meet again in the Hall, for we are spent with weariness and soiled with travel."

With another touch of his mother's hand, Robin left the company and went to find Brother Luke and to make himself ready for the audience.

There never was such merrymaking as took place in the Hall that Christmas Eve. Such ballads sung! Such tales told!

Branches of holly and spruce decked the Hall and filled the air with fragrance. The yule log burned on the hearth and flaming torches filled the sconces.

The King and Queen sat enthroned in the great chairs on the dais. A tapestry was draped on the screen behind them and rich Eastern carpets beneath.

Sir Peter and Lady Constance sat at one side of the King and Queen and Sir John and Lady Maud at the other.

Robin entered the Hall with Brother Luke as he had been commanded, and at a signal came forward to stand before the dais. He wore a black velvet doublet and carried the Saxon harp on his back. As usual, D'Ath followed at his heels.

Robin felt as though the Hall were as long as London Bridge, for when he entered all was quiet, and his crutches seemed to make a great sound on the stone floor. Servants and courtiers bowed as he passed.

What was going to happen?

What had the King to say to him? Would his parents leave him and go back to London?

At last he reached the dais. The King rose and stood over Robin, lifting from his own shoulders a chain of gold set with medallions of fine workmanship, then he spoke.

"Can you kneel, my son?" he asked.

"I can for a little time, Sire," answered Robin, "long enough to say 'Our Father'." He dropped to the cushion, supporting himself with one crutch. The friar took the other.

"Robin, son of Sir John de Bureford," the King said solemnly, "it hath been told to us what service you have done for the lord of this castle and me, King of the whole realm of England and France. You are a true son of a noble father. Though but a youth, you have shown courage a man might be proud to call his own."

The King spread out the jeweled collar and dropped it onto Robin's shoulders, saying, "This shall be a token of our high regard and with it go our grateful thanks.

"Rise, young Robin," he commanded, and himself raised Robin to his feet.

Robin was filled with gratitude to the King, because now his father could be proud of him. He could not speak for a moment, and indeed knew of nothing to say. But cheers and hand clapping began to make such a noise and clatter that no speech could have been heard.

When the noise had quieted a little, Robin was quieter, too. He remembered the carol he had been learning for this very night, and words came to him.

"Sire," Robin began, "I do thank you for this great honor, and I beg you to accept my song of Christmas." He brought forward the little harp he had grown to love and sang this carol:

Come to Bethlehem and see
Him whose birth the angels sing;
Come, adore on bended knee,
Christ the Lord, the new-born King.
Gloria in excelsis Deo
Gloria in excelsis Deo.

When the song was ended, once more the Hall rang with shouts and cheers. "Sir Robin! Sir Robin!" Robin found himself standing between his mother and his father.

Sir Robin. Was it *he*?

"Sir," he addressed his father, "mind you not that I must go thus, bent over, and with these crutches to help me walk?" For he must know the worst at once.

Gravely Sir John answered, "The courage you have shown, the craftsmanship proven by the harp, and the spirit in your singing all make so bright a light that I cannot see whether or no your legs are misshapen."

"As for me," said Lady Maud, slipping her arm about Robin, "what a comfort it will be to know that wars will never claim you. And you can come home, for there is now no need for you to stay here at Lindsay. Nor is there further need for me to be with the Queen. She is now in good health. When the Feast of Christmas is over, we shall all go home to London. Brother Luke shall come with us to be your tutor, if he will."

When the midnight office was said in the church, the whole household trooped back to the Hall, where tables were spread for the feast. Platters were heaped with food and carried in by pages and esquires. A giant boar's head came first in order, then pasties and whole suckling pigs, pigeons and geese roasted with feathers on. The meats were followed by flaming puddings and bowls of wassail, chestnuts, and apples.

D'Ath and the other hounds feasted, too, for all the scraps were thrown into the rushes on the floor.

It was nearly dawn when Robin felt himself lifted onto Brother Luke's back, for he had fallen asleep.

"Where am I?" he asked in bewilderment. "What has happened?"

"Thou'rt here, Sir Robin," said the friar. "Safe with all thy loved ones. 'Tis the Feast of Christmas, and thou hast found the door in thy wall."